Festival of Feelings

Paige Skinner

Contents

Chapter 1

It's been exactly three years since the last time I saw Ty Rossi, and let me tell you, it hasn't been long enough.

I snap the pool house door shut behind me and hustle across my aunt's backyard. We haven't gotten around to cutting the grass this week, and the long blades swish against the leather of my vintage boots. The sound of familiar voices and splashing drowns out the chirping of crickets. The party is already in full swing, which means I am so screwed.

Craning my neck, I scan the line of cars parked out front, but I don't see Ty's old, red pickup anywhere. That does little to untangle the knot of nerves, which has been lodged in my gut since I heard he was back in town.

I shake out my arms like a fighter about to enter the ring. I can handle this.

I'm less than thrilled about throwing this little shindig since it almost certainly means coming face-to-face with my ex. But my cousin, Liv, just got home from a semester at Brown University, and she's been so excited to host this mini-reunion. I didn't want to crap all over her fun.

And I do have to admit, it looks pretty great back here. Between the twinkly lights and the citrusy-sweet scent of Aunt Betty's honeysuckle vines, it's like a proper country garden party. If you overlook the massive jug of jungle juice and guest list comprised of my barely legal, former classmates, that is.

Liv has an old Taylor Swift bop blaring through a pair of speakers next to the pool. The bass rattles the concrete as I hustle behind the table of snacks she's set up. I open a bag of chips and dump it into an empty bowl as though I've totally been here, playing hostess all night like I was supposed to be.

Liv's going to be beyond angry with me. Not that I can blame her. I mean, what kind of jerk shows up late to a party at their own house?

Oh, yeah. That would be me.

Glancing around, I try to spot her in the crowd. It's like being sucked into a time warp. The faces are the same but also different somehow. Like someone's put an Instagram filter over the pages of my old yearbook. The haircuts have changed, and the Rosedale High liger that used to be plastered across everyone's T-shirts has been replaced with various university logos.

I'm not sad to see Larry the Liger fade into memory. Because let's be real, having a liger for a mascot is cheesy even by Rosedale standards. It's like the student body couldn't choose between a lion and a tiger and somehow decided a liger was a solid compromise. All the college paraphernalia is a little overkill, though. In a town of three thousand people, even Old Man Jenkins remembers which schools everyone got into.

"Kallie, I just watched you take two shots of tequila. So if you haven't done a back handspring in three years, then maybe don't." I hear Liv's irritated voice from the other side of the yard, where some of our former cheerleaders are attempting tumbling passes.

"Every party has a pooper," Kallie singsongs. She's exceptionally tan in her white cutoffs, considering it's only the first of June. She's taking full advantage of the fact that her mom owns the town's only beauty salon and tanning bed.

"I swear to God. If I have to get an ambulance to scrape your drunk butt off my lawn again, I will call your mother," Liv says.

Wonderful. She's already in a mood, and the odds that she hasn't noticed my tardiness are currently sitting around zero. Liv might be my best friend/cousin, but she takes crap from nobody, including me.

I'm astonished Kallie can feel anything through her alcohol-induced stupor, but miraculously, she must sense my gaze on them. She looks over at me and loudly shout-slurs, "Quinn's here! Hiiii, Quinn!"

Based on her unprecedented levels of enthusiasm, you'd think we'd been besties forever. In reality, we barely say hi when we cross paths in town. Which is unfortunate since, unlike most of our graduating class, neither of us went away to college. Kallie, because she's training to take over her mom's salon. Me, because...well, reasons.

I cringe as Liv whirls around. Her blue glare is glacial enough to give a person frostbite despite the humid air. She clocks my YouTube-tutorial-worthy makeup. My shimmery gold eyeshadow is the exact same shade as my ponytail. And I ironed the paisley shirt dress I'm wearing precisely seven times before setting foot outside the door.

Liv raises an eyebrow in an arch so fierce it manages to communicate all the many words she'd be saying—nay, yelling—if the entirety of Rosedale High's class of 2020 wasn't standing in our yard.

Sorry, I mouth and grimace apologetically. Liv just shakes her head before turning her attention back to Kallie, who looks like she's about to go in for a roundoff.

I press a hand to my neck, which I'm sure is going all red and splotchy like it does anytime I feel upset, embarrassed, or, yeah, guilty. If I were Liv, I'd be mad too. This isn't the first time I've been late to something because I was attempting to vanquish any potential flaws in my appearance. Which, believe you me, is not a personality trait I'm proud of.

But the way I look is one of the few things in my life I can actually control, so control it I do. Especially when I'm stressed or something unexpected happens, i.e., my ex-boyfriend randomly coming back to our small town for summer break.

"So, did you fall into a sinkhole on your way to the party?" Liv strides over to the table, hand popped on the hip of her romper. She always dresses head-to-toe in black in this witchy, cowgirl aesthetic that I wish I could pull off.

I sigh, fiddling with the hem of my dress. "N—"

Liv doesn't let me finish. "Have to sacrifice a virgin to the Dark Lord before you could leave?"

"Well—"

"Accidentally flood the pool house again? Because I know you have a really good reason for being over an hour late."

"Okay, that was one time. And Liv, I'm so sorry. It wasn't intentional. I just—" I sputter, heat searing up my chest and neck again. "You know, with him coming back to town. I got...stuck in my head." I bite the inside of my cheek because my eyes are burning now too, and I am not about to get emotional in the middle of this party. Not over a guy I broke up with literal years ago.

Liv scrunches her lips to the side, fire fading from her eyes. If anyone understands why I'm the way that I am, Liv does. "Fine. But you're making me a very, very big batch of brownies tomorrow."

I raise my hand. "I swear. I'll even use real sugar."

This is truly a selfless act since chocolate is my life's blood, and I can't eat sugar. A lick of that batter would mean spending the rest of the day with a migraine and a glorious collection of hives. Thank you, food allergies.

Liv's mouth kicks up in a smirk. "You drive a hard bargain, Quinn Kelly. Now make yourself useful." She jerks her chin toward the massive—and nearly empty—jug of jungle juice. "Apparently, everyone's chosen binge drinking as their major." She rolls her eyes.

Liv takes her education seriously. She's getting her degree in psychology, so she can become a relationship counselor after she graduates. I have no doubt she'll be running her own practice in no time.

I grab one of the bottles of rum Liv "borrowed" from Aunt Betty's liquor cabinet and start glugging it into the pitcher.

"Quinn's drinking now? Alright!" A pale, freckled hand plants itself in front of my face for a high-five. I glance up to find Chance Sparrow squinting down at me, eyes struggling to focus. He's paired his old Carhartt jeans with a University of Tennessee T-shirt, which he's already spilled something on. His tomato-red hair is a hot mess.

My stomach dips, and my eyes flick past Chance's shoulder to the group of guys standing in a drunken cluster next to the table. The tall, dark, and infuriatingly handsome face I'm looking for is notably absent. I release a breath, and my internal organs manage to right themselves.

"Still not drinking. Just playing bartender." I force myself to smile even though my jaw is clenched hard enough to crack. Having to constantly explain my diet to people is exhausting. It's not like I have any choice in the matter. And seeing Chance when he's home for break is like sprinkling salt over a years-old wound that won't heal. He played a big role in the fight that ended my relationship with Ty.

The song changes to "Dancin' In The Country" by Tyler Hubbard. Chance whoops, turning back to his bro squad, who start jumping up and down.

The lines once so strictly drawn between cliques have been magically erased since we graduated. Kelvin—football star—gives Evan—debate club president—a hearty clap on the back, sending him stumbling. Evan ricochets off the table, taking out one of the legs in the process, and landing in a giggling heap on the cement.

Bowls of chips and Hot Cheetos go soaring as the jungle juice tips forward, toppling from the table and shattering against the pavement. Squealing, I try to jump out of the way, but there's no avoiding the remaining alcohol as it splashes over my feet, probably ruining my favorite boots. The sharp, acrid smell of it burns my nose.

"Kelvin, you idiot!" I yell, smacking him on a bicep that's only gotten meatier since the last time I saw him.

"What did I do? Harper's the one who knocked it over." He jerks his chin toward Evan, who's still curled in a ball, laughing while I'm trying and utterly failing to see the humor in the situation.

"Yeah, because you were acting like a goon like always," Liv snaps. She bends down and carefully plucks pieces of glass off the concrete before depositing them in the garbage can.

"Aww, don't be like that," Chance slurs, coming to Kelvin's defense as per usual.

I roll my eyes. There's no point talking to Chance and Kelvin basically ever, but especially after they've engaged drunken-dope mode.

"I'll go get the broom," I mutter to Liv.

She nods, shooting another death glare in Chance and Kelvin's direction. They're standing next to the pool, whispering to each other like preteens at a sleepover.

Fuming, I turn toward the kitchen, but Chance lunges forward, stumbling into my path. "Quinn, don't leave like this."

"Move." I give him a flat look.

"Let us make it up to you," Kelvin calls from behind me.

"By actually cleaning up after yourselves for once?" I sidestep Chance, who tries to block me but trips over his own stupid feet, almost face-planting.

"Oh, we'll help you clean up, alright," Kelvin says.

Before I can ask what he means by that, his arm is clinched around my waist, hoisting me into the air and over his shoulder.

"What do you think you're doing?" I shout, flailing my legs wildly and kicking at him. He might be wrecked, but he's still maddeningly coordinated, easily holding me at an angle so I can't inflict any damage. I can't tell if the pounding in my head is from all the blood rushing to it or my fury over Kelvin picking me up without my permission.

"We're helping you wash up." Kelvin struts across the patio. His heavy footsteps rumble through me, making my teeth clatter.

"Put me down!" I hammer his back with my fists.

"You asked for it." Kelvin takes a running step forward. I realize what he's going to do a second before it happens.

"Kelvin, don't you da—" My voice cuts off in a shriek as Kelvin launches me into the pool, flawless hair, pristine dress, boots, and all.

Chapter 2

My boots are so heavy they might as well be filled with cement. I struggle to the pool's surface, dress tangling around my thighs.

I am going to murder Kelvin Jones.

My head breaks the water, and I gasp, sucking in air. Water flies in all directions as I flail my arms like a drunken ballerina. I've been borderline obsessed with these vintage, second-hand boots ever since I first spotted them in the window of Miss Jenny's Boutique. But now I realize they're death traps. The longer I'm in the water, the more of it they absorb. They're getting heavier by the second.

I'm so mad; my hands shake as they thrash through the water. But what pisses me off most is that I should have been expecting Chance and Kelvin to pull something like this. It's like high school all over again. Just with their ringleader, Ty, mysteriously absent.

I reach down, desperately tugging at one of my boots. My foot manages to slip free, but my head submerges again in the process, and I inhale half the pool.

The hot-pink pool light sears my eyes. Spots dance in my vision as I surface, coughing up a lungful of water. "Kel...cough...vin! You're...cough...dead!"

But between my splashing and the verbal smack-down Liv's serving him, Kelvin can't hear me. He's standing at the pool's edge with Chance, hunched over and laughing so hard it looks like he's about to pee himself.

Ooooh. White, hot fury floods through me. I finally wriggle out of my other boot and focus all my energy on flinging it over my head at Kelvin. I hear a wet whump followed by his yelp of surprise before my head bobs back under the choppy waves I've created with all my thrashing. Well, if I'm about to drown, at least I'll die having exacted my revenge.

The tang of chlorine burns my nose. I fight back to the surface, heaving in gulps of the heavy air. Without the cinder blocks strapped to my feet, I can finally kick my legs. My dress appears to be in cahoots with my homicidal footwear, though. It drags in the water, trying to pull me back to the depths.

Everyone has gathered around the pool. Most of them are clearly Team Kelvin, laughing right along with him. But a few people are hovering around the ledge like they might actually care whether I sink into an early grave. None of them bother getting in to help me, though.

I growl in frustration and embarrassment. Thrusting my arms out in front of me, I send a wave of water toward Chance and Kelvin. It doesn't come close to hitting them, and they just laugh harder.

They'd better be able to run. Because if I ever make it out of this pool, I swear to the lord above, it's the death for both of them.

I stretch out my fingertips, but I'm still shy of reaching the edge. Giving one final kick, I propel myself forward. Before I can grasp the concrete, though, a hand wraps around my upper arm, pulling me to safety.

I cling to the ledge, bare legs dangling in the water. My dress floats around my hips, and I'm positive my banana-yellow underwear is on full display. I'm having a hard time caring, though. Because that hand is still on my arm. I know that hand—long fingers, warm skin, and nights spent getting lost in the back of a pickup truck.

The knees of his faded blue jeans are damp from where he's kneeling next to the pool. My eyes travel up, taking in his wavy dark hair, strong jaw, and lips like a fairy tale. The cut of his shoulders is much broader than the last time I saw him. Heart walloping against my sternum, I force myself to meet his deep brown gaze. It's first love and heartbreak, and a rush of emotions so complicated and intense it makes my stomach swoop like I'm a passenger on a plummeting airplane, bracing for the inevitable impact of the crash.

"Ty." His name is familiar on my tongue, cinnamon and honey.

"Quinn, are you okay?" His voice thrums through me like someone plucked the strings of my heart. He places his hands on my waist, easily lifting me from the water. "What happened?"

"I'm fine." I tug at the sopping-wet hem of my dress. It's like I've got a weighted blanket hanging from my shoulders. "Your idiot friends thought throwing me in the pool would be fun."

"Seriously?" Ty's eyes widen as he turns to Kelvin and Chance. "You two must have a death wish." He nods toward Liv. Her arms are crossed over her chest, fingernails digging into her skin like it's taking every ounce of self-control she possesses not to throttle them.

The corner of Ty's mouth twitches, sparking the temper I'm barely keeping in check. Of course, he'd find this situation entertaining. He always had to be the class clown. The funny guy. This is exactly the kind of thing he used to do when we were together. He'd pull some stupid prank for a laugh, no matter the consequences. Forget the fact that I have a dumb chronic condition that makes me low-key allergic to just about everything, including chlorine.

"It's not funny," I snap, twisting out of his grip.

Ty's attention flicks back to me. His lips part in surprise. "Hey, I didn't say it w—"

"And I don't need Liv to fight my battles for me. I'm not weak." I rub my fingertips across my face, trying to scrub away the streaks of mascara staining my cheeks.

I might have been sick back when Ty and I dated, but that was before I got my diagnosis for MCAS—Mast Cell Activation Syndrome—and got my life under control. I'm not that girl anymore. I am more than capable of taking care of myself.

"I know that." His eyes skate over my body. "You look good, Quinn. Healthy."

The logical part of my brain recognizes that he means that as a compliment. Unfortunately, the logic train left the station the second Kelvin launched me into the pool. Seeing Ty for the first time since we broke up with makeup running down my face when he looks like he just walked out of a Calvin Klein ad isn't helping either.

"I look good? I look like a cat someone drowned in the bathtub." My hands curl into fists as water runs down my arms, pooling on the patio.

Ty darts a glance around the party. I'm aware that all our former classmates are staring at us, hanging on our every word. Their laughter and chatter from earlier has come to a crashing halt.

Ty and I seeing each other for the first time in years is headline-worthy news in Rosedale. But the weight of everyone's attention only makes me angrier. Luckily, being mad is easier than trying to sort through my mess of emotions over being this close to Ty after all these years. I cling to that anger like a life jacket.

"So, did you put your boys up to this?" I demand, shoving away the wet strands of hair that stick to my neck.

"Are you kidding?" Ty throws his hands up, clearly exasperated with me. "Quinn, I just got here. I was trying to help you."

"Well, it isn't like you haven't done anything like this before." I blink my eyes, the chlorine already making them itch. This argument feels all too familiar. Like we're following a script we wrote back in high school and haven't figured out how to edit.

Ty barks out a humorless laugh, scrubbing his palms over his face. "You can't seriously still be mad at me. That was years ago, Quinn."

"And yet, you still haven't apologized."

Ty risked my entire future with the last prank he pulled when we were together. Time might have a way of making past hurts feel less significant, but that's only until they come storming back into your life and plucking you out of swimming pools. I don't think I even realized how mad I still am until I saw him tonight.

Ty bites his lips together like he's thinking hard about the next words that are going to come out of his mouth. He leans toward me, and I can smell his cologne, crisp and woodsy. He drops his voice, "You need to calm down so we can talk, okay?"

I don't know how much Ty pays UCLA for tuition, but whatever it is, it's too much. He's obviously learned nothing in the last three years if he thinks telling someone to 'calm down' is a smart thing to do.

I glance from his face—just inches from my own—to the heels of his own worn leather boots. He's standing directly in front of the pool's edge. Ty's eyes narrow in suspicion as I flash him a smile as sweet as the sugar I can't eat. I set a hand in the center of his chest. It's much more muscular than I remember. So I put all my strength into it as I shove him backward into the water.

Chapter 3

Here's the thing about Rosedale, it's so charming it should be annoying. But from the picket fences to the cobblestone streets that turn into dirt roads as they wind their way out of town, I'm completely in love with the place. It's predictable, and sure, it can be a little boring. But I'm here for it. In my opinion, people severely underrate the value of predictability. Clearly, they've never had to live without it.

I fell head-over-heels with this town the day Aunt Betty invited me to stay with them during my sophomore year of high school. After graduation, I moved from her guest bedroom to the pool house. I'll probably live there until I'm forty since the prescription I need to control my MCAS costs more than most people's mortgages, and my dad's insurance only pays for part of it. Forget renting a place of my own. Forget college. But honestly, I wouldn't leave Rosedale even if I could afford it.

It doesn't appear my beloved cobblestones feel quite the same way about me, though. The second I step off the sidewalk in front of Nelson's Bakery, one of the little monsters tries to murder me. I can't see where I'm stepping over my tote bag full of cookbooks, my Stanley cup, and the giant box of fresh-baked triple-chocolate-chunk cookies I'm schlepping across town. My foot comes down unevenly, sending me stumbling.

The bag of cookbooks topples out of my arms, and my Stanley hits the road with a clang so loud it's like someone rang the bells in the church spire. It rolls down the uneven street, making an unholy clatter as it goes. The box of cookies teeters dangerously. I have a second of pure panic, imagining a grisly scene of chocolate and crumbs smeared across the road before I manage to clamp my hands around it. The edges are crumpled, but it's intact.

After my Oscar-worthy exit from the party last night, I owe Liv more than a batch of the Paleo brownies I'm making for my baking class this morning. The triple-chocolate-chunk cookies from Nelson's are her favorite. Unfortunately, everyone else in Rosedale agrees. They rarely make it through the morning. Since the class I'm teaching doesn't end until after eleven, I didn't want to risk it.

Concentrating on not dropping the now-mangled box of cookies, I hoist my tote bag safely over my arm. I turn to chase down my cup and nearly smack into a t-shirt-clad chest that's entirely too familiar.

"I think this belongs to you."

I stare at the hand holding my hot-pink Stanley and groan. I don't know what I've done to anger the fates this week, but they definitely have it out for me. Because that hand is the same one that pulled me from the pool last night, and I am not in the mood for it.

No one should have to untangle their jumbled-up emotions over their ex before noon, especially if they didn't get enough sleep the night before. Even after showering, I was awake for hours with my skin itching and eyes burning from chlorine.

"I'm pretty sure what you meant to say was, 'Thank you so much, Ty.' An apology for pushing me in the pool wouldn't hurt either." Ty's lips quirk in a self-satisfied smirk.

"Wouldn't hurt you, maybe." I try to snatch the cup from his grip and almost drop the cookies again.

"Wow." Ty holds the cup above his head, out of my reach. "You really suck at apologies."

"You're one to talk." I glare up at him, squinting in the hazy morning sunshine. His white shirt clings to the muscles of his biceps. And lord knows why, but he's wearing an actual tool belt, which is slightly hot and seriously irritating. He's like the Italian version of one of the freaking Property Brothers.

I lunge for my Hydro Flask again, but Ty easily dodges me.

Heat prickles at my neck and chest. I try to reel in my irritation before I turn into the human equivalent of a lobster. "You know what, keep it." I spin on my heel and stomp across the street, ducking through the line of maple trees surrounding the park.

Rosedale is starting to wake up. A group of middle-school boys throws a football back and forth. The scent of roasting coffee beans wafts from the cart on the corner. The sprinklers must have just turned off because chilly drops of water speckle my ankles as I cut through the grass. Ty's boots squeak behind me, and I can feel the weight of his eyes against my skin.

I give my ponytail a flip and, okay, maybe put a little extra oomph in my swagger. But can you blame me? Last night was the first time I'd seen Ty since graduation, and I looked like a swamp rat. My appearance this morning is a drastic improvement, which I realize is a low bar. But if I'm being honest, Ty looks good. Really good. Time has chiseled his features, making him look older and more mature.

Even if I don't want to date him ever again, I can't help wanting him to think that I look good too.

I spent way too long applying my neutral-toned makeup. It both matches my cropped tee and looks totally natural. The effort had nothing to do with Ty, though. Well, it wasn't entirely to do with Ty. Thanks to the skylights, the classroom at Giselle's Gourmet Cooking School has excellent lighting, and I need to get some photos for my Instagram account.

I'm finishing my certification, so I can become an online nutrition counselor for people with health conditions like mine. And if I want to run an online company, I need to have a solid social media presence. I'm constantly sharing healthy recipes and baking tips. My goal is to have over twenty-five thousand followers by the end of the summer. I'll need a large audience when I launch my company. Helping other people achieve wellness is my dream.

As is having my ex-boyfriend crawl back to wherever he came from. I can still hear him hot on my heels.

"Quinn, come on. Wait up," Ty calls after me. "At least take your girly water bottle back."

"No, thanks." I don't break my stride.

"You're being stubborn."

"You're being annoying, but you don't hear me complaining." I pick up the pace, speed-walking toward the old barn Giselle converted into a cooking classroom.

She lets me teach modified baking classes several times a week and pays me way too much. The turnout for my courses is practically non-existent, especially compared to the crowds Giselle draws for her gourmet cooking classes. Her wife has a chronic health condition, though, so I think she's got a soft spot for me. My classes are geared toward helping people comply with dietary restrictions. All my recipes are either Paleo, sugar-free, AIP, or Keto-friendly. I'm like the all-inclusive resort of baking instructors.

The cooking school's on the far edge of town. But when I reach the reclaimed wooden steps out front, Ty's right behind me.

I whirl around. "Why are you following me?"

"Believe it or not, not everything's about you. I'm working here." Ty drops my cup on top of the cardboard box I'm holding, caving in the lid and, I'm sure, squashing the cookies.

"What do you mean you're working here?" I don't know if it's just really hot or if my blood is actually boiling. Ty's lucky my arms are full.

"I'm helping Al with the remodel."

I was so focused on Ty I didn't notice the cacophony of hammers and drills coming from inside the school. Crap. I forgot they were starting construction today. Giselle's adding another room. She keeps saying it's because her classes are getting too big. But since the population of Rosedale hasn't grown since I moved here, I strongly suspect it's so I can keep teaching classes while she's doing hers in the other room.

"Why are you helping Al?" I ask. "You don't even live here."

"It's called a summer job. Besides, I thought some hands-on experience would help me with my courses this semester." Ty's studying architecture, so it makes sense, which doesn't make it any less irritating. "And I just went away to college," he continues. "It isn't like I don't live here anymore."

"Could've fooled me."

"What's that supposed to mean?" Ty's leaning toward me, and my pulse is thrumming at the closeness. Every cell in my body screams at me to put some space between us, but I'm not about to back down.

I shrug like I couldn't care less. "I just didn't think you were the kind of guy to forget where he came from. But you haven't bothered to visit once in the last three years."

Pink splotches appear on Ty's cheeks. I'm definitely getting under his skin. "This town is my home. I was born here. I've got roots. You'll always just be the new girl." He says that last bit with so much superiority it makes my fingers curl around the cookie box, denting the lid even more.

I narrow my eyes at him. "And you're a—"

The white-washed barn door slides open, old wheels squeaking and cutting off my sentence. I jump as Giselle pokes her head out. Her shiny, dark hair is pulled back in a tight bun, highlighting her perfect cheekbones and flawless complexion. She's like a Brazilian Gal Gadot.

"I thought I heard voices. What are you doing out here?" she asks, a hint of an accent curling the edges of her words. Then her wide, brown eyes land on Ty, and she breaks into a mega-watt smile. "Ty! Welcome home!" She rushes down the steps and envelops him in a hug.

I roll my eyes as Ty hugs her back.

"It's been too long," Giselle steps back, holding him at arm's length to examine him. "And I swear you've gotten even taller."

Ty ducks his head, grinning and looking embarrassed. "It has been too long." He shoots a pointed look in my direction. "But it's expensive to fly across the country when you're also paying student loans."

Giselle tuts. "It's criminal how much they charge you kids for tuition."

"No arguments here," Ty says, still glaring at me. I glower right back at him. Giselle isn't wrong, but she's also unknowingly fighting—and winning—Ty's argument for him. I set what's left of Liv's cookies on the ground and cross my arms over my chest, waiting for the two of them to wrap up their little reunion.

"Al's out back," Giselle tells Ty. "Work hard, so you can come home sooner next time."

Ty's eyes fall to the pavement, and his smile falters. "Yeah. I'll, uh, I'll do that." He scrubs his hand over the back of his neck in that way he used to when he was either lying or trying to hide some ridiculous scheme he'd come up with—usually with the help of his bonehead friends.

I wonder what that's all about. Before I can say anything, a freshly waxed, antique pickup truck pulls up to the curb. Giselle's wife, Paula, climbs out, looking visibly shaken. Her usually immaculate blond pixie cut is rumpled like she's been running her hands through it, and her face is flushed. Her suit is disheveled, like she got dressed in a hurry.

It's out of character for Paula to be anything but confident and collected. Seeing her like this makes my heart beat double-time. Something must be seriously wrong. People call her the Queen of the North around here. Not only because she's the mayor and her house is at the north end of town, but because she's a total boss. I'd bend the knee to Paula. She's always quick to put a council member in their place during town meetings. She's also a commercial banker by day, who fights to get funding for women in business.

"What happened?" Giselle releases Ty's arm and rushes over to Paula.

"It's Mom." Paula combs one hand through her hair while typing frantically at her phone with the other. "She fell. They rushed her to the hospital. It sounds like she's broken her hip."

Giselle gasps and wraps her arms around Paula. "What can I do?"

Paula leans into her. "I don't know yet. I'm booking a flight now, so I can be with her."

"Do you want me to go with you?" Giselle sets her palm against Paula's cheek.

"No." Paula shakes her head. "I'm sure she's going to be fine. She'll probably just need help for a few weeks. Besides, you've got too much going on between the festival and all this." She gestures toward the school, where the construction team's hard at work.

"I didn't think about the festival. Can someone fill in for you?" Giselle's eyes are tight with concern.

Paula sighs, her hands falling to her sides. "I messaged everyone on the council. They're being unsurprisingly useless."

Rosedale's Founder's Festival is scheduled to kick off on Sunday. It's a week-long celebration with a different town activity happening each night. From what Giselle's told me, Paula's been working on it almost non-stop for the past couple of months. Having the festival without Paula here is like The Beatles going on tour without John. It'll be a complete circus.

"I don't mean to interrupt." Ty takes a step toward Paula and Giselle. "But I'd be happy to help with the festival."

Ty's being thoughtful, which is a good thing. I'm aware of that. But him jumping in and offering to help before I did flips some illogically competitive switch inside my head. Paula and Giselle are my friends. And this is my town. If anyone should be helping, it's me.

"Yes. Paula, what do you need?" I ask, stepping deliberately in front of Ty. I can feel the blaze of his irritation radiating off of him.

Paula glances between us, looking both confused and apprehensive. "Someone's going to need to run the Founder's Festival while I'm gone. Do you think you could manage it?"

"Of course," I say at the same time Ty says, "Absolutely." We exchange scowls before turning back to Paula. The skin between her eyebrows puckers in confusion. Her eyes flick over to Giselle, who shrugs as though saying, you don't have any better options.

Paula's teeth worry her lip as she studies us. "The two of you would be doing me a huge favor. It would be a lot of work, though. And Giselle will be busy catering the food for the events. Are you sure you're up to it?"

I would rather run naked through the town square than work with Ty on anything. But I owe Giselle and Paula so much. Being there for them is much more important than our drama.

I open my mouth to say as much, but Ty cuts me off.

"I'd do anything to help you, Paula." He looks over at me. "And my town."

I bite my cheek to keep myself from saying anything snarky to him. Because the groove between Paula's brows is getting deeper, and she's already got enough on her plate.

I force a bright smile. "We'll take care of everything."

"Alright." Paula's shoulders rise and fall with a heavy breath. "I really appreciate this. Quinn, I know you have classes this morning. So, Ty, if you want to come with me, we can stop by my office to grab everything you'll need before I leave for the airport."

"No problem. Let me tell Al where I'm going." His eyes lock on mine as he strides past. "And I'll see you later, partner." He winks at me.

Someone must have set the dial on my emotions to hot mess. Because that wink triggers a flood of memories of all the times he winked at me like that when we were together. It made me melt like honey on a gluten-free biscuit every time. Part of me wants to swoon. The other, more rational part wants to kick him in the shin.

I squeeze my eyes shut, dragging in a breath through my nose. It'll be a miracle if Ty and I both survive the week.

Chapter 4

"Hello?" I edge the kitchen door of the main house open with my hip, holding the mangled cookie box in my hands.

Calling it the main house makes it sound fancier than it is—especially when Aunt Betty says it in her Downton Abbey accent. We just started referring to it that way when I moved into the pool house. Don't get me wrong. It's a lovely home, craftsman-style with a wrap-around porch and blue-shuttered windows. But Rosedale is a pretty stereotypical working-class suburb. Betty might be an M.D., but she makes a fraction of what most doctors do.

She specializes in a holistic approach and owns her own practice. She'll spend hours with one patient, helping them figure out whatever's ailing them. She only charges people what they can afford. She advocates for universal health care and always speaks out about how it should be free for everyone.

Preach, sister. Preach.

"In here," Liv calls from the front room.

I kick off my shoes, sparing a moment of silence for my ruined boots. Pushing the door shut with my hip, I pad across the cool tile floor. The kitchen is pristine, all stainless steel and shiny sur-faces—not because Betty and Liv are amazing housekeepers but because no one ever cooks here. In contrast, the buttery-yellow walls of the hallway are cluttered with photographs.

"Hey, Mom," I whisper like I always do when I pass a picture of us with Olivia and Betty at the county fair. It was taken the summer before Mom died. Her arms are around me, and we're all smiling hugely. From our matching single dimples to our round eyes, every-one says I'm my mom's mini-me. I think she looked more like Betty, though. Betty's hair is a dark chestnut, and my mom was a golden blond. Other than that, they were identical.

Liv's sprawled out on the red leather sofa, fanning herself with a magazine when I walk into the living room. There's a collection of tabloids on the old oak coffee table. The television is turned off for once, and Betty's sitting cross-legged in front of the built-in bookcase that overflows with her collection of VHS tapes and old Babysitter's Club paperbacks. I don't know another person who still owns VHS tapes, but that's Betty.

She's studying one of the magazine's crinkly pages. She glances up at me as I walk in. A mischievous grin stretches across her face. "Excuse me, miss. But do you have a moment to talk about our lord and savior, Zac Efron?" She flips the tabloid around with a flourish, revealing a full-page spread of the Zefron on a white, sandy beach.

"You know I only worship one man, my sweet Baby Hemsworth." I drop the cookies on the stack of magazines and flop back on my favorite squashy armchair. The fabric is worn from years of use.

"Amen." Liv swings her legs over the side of the couch, knocking a throw pillow to the floor as she sits up.

Betty gasps. "Blasphemous, children."

"Please tell me those are what I think they are." Liv points at the box of cookies. Her hair is up in a messy ponytail that manages to look both effortless and on-trend.

"If you think they're triple-chocolate-chunk cookies to bribe you for your forgiveness, then yes."

Liv squeals and lunges for the box.

"Wow, bribery cookies," Betty says. "What did you do?"

"Other than showing up late to Liv's party and pushing one of her guests in the pool, nothing." I shrug.

Betty nods, eyebrows raised in appreciation. "And the Academy Award goes to..."

"We're living with a regular Bette Davis over here." Liv shimmies the lid off the box and pauses. "Ummm, why are my apology cookies mutilated?"

I wince. "Would you believe me if I told you Nelson's is trying something new? Cookie crumbs. You know, like donut holes."

Liv does that eyebrow arch thing that I can't master, no matter how many hours I waste attempting to replicate it in my bathroom mirror.

Dropping my head back against the chair cushion, I groan. "Fine. You can thank Ty. He's what happened to your cookies."

"Ty? As in Ty Rossi?" Betty leans forward eagerly, elbows resting on the table.

"The one and only. He's home for the summer." I suck in a breath through my nose, inhaling the homey smell of Betty's country-apple candle.

"Ah. I'm gonna go out on a limb and guess he was the guest you pushed in the pool."

"I'm exercising my fifth amendment right to stay silent and protect the innocent, AKA myself."

Liv climbs to her feet. "I'm getting a spoon. I won't be deterred from devouring these cookies, crumbs and all."

"Loving your dedication," Betty calls after her as she pads toward the kitchen. "So," she turns to me, "can we expect a production every time you run into Ty this summer? Because if so, I'll get my popcorn ready."

I prop an elbow on the arm of the chair, leaning my head against my hand. "Is it wrong if you want to punch your ex-boyfriend in the face whenever you see them?"

"Honey, if that's wrong, then I don't want to be right." Betty shoves a handful of cookie crumbs in her mouth. "Why do you think I refuse to commit to a relationship status?"

Betty loves men. Dating them. Falling in love with them. But she loathes the idea of monogamous relationships. She said she tried it once in high school, and it wasn't for her. Betty was on a date with her latest man-friend last night; she thinks the word 'boyfriend' implies too much commitment. Which is why she missed the reunion episode of the Quinn and Ty show. For Betty, the best part of a relationship is always the beginning when you're all googly eyes and butterfly-filled stomachs.

While I respect that, I disagree. I think the greatest parts are when you're so comfortable with the other person you can be your true self. When you don't care if they see you in a messy bun and no makeup. When you know them so well, you can guess what they'll order at every restaurant and how they'll finish their sentences. I love the monotony of knowing what our plans will be every Friday night and having someone to depend on. I miss it.

"So, since we're talking about menfolk," Betty says, "your dad called."

"Of course he did." I sigh, but it's out of a fond kind of exasperation. I FaceTime my Dad daily, but he never believes I'm doing okay health-wise until he talks to Betty. I can't really blame him.

After my mom's car accident, my health spiraled, which isn't uncommon. Underlying chronic conditions are frequently triggered by grief. But MCAS isn't well-known, and it's difficult to diagnose. We saw nearly every specialist in New York City before Dad finally caved and sent me to Betty. He thought holistic medicine was too 'woo woo' back then. It took five years of me being sick and miserable before he was willing to let Betty try. Five. Years.

Betty was the only doctor to think outside the box enough to do the proper testing and get me a diagnosis. Her combination of traditional medication and changes to my diet and lifestyle have made all the difference—coming to live with Betty and Liv being one of those lifestyle changes. The crappy air in New York triggers my flare-ups, and since there isn't much demand for people who work in marketing here in Rosedale, Dad couldn't leave his job in the city.

"I told him you were doing great because you are, kid." Betty smiles warmly at me.

Her words give me that warm, snuggly feeling I used to get when my mom hugged me. "Thanks, Betty."

"So what do you think? Margaritas or Cape Cods?" Liv walks back into the room. She's holding two spoons, one bottle of tequila, and a bottle of vodka. She plops back down on the sofa, setting her goods on the table.

"Why not both?" Betty asks.

"It isn't even noon yet." I laugh. Betty may be a doctor, but that doesn't mean she's a healthy eater. Chronic illnesses run in families. My mom and grandmother both had Hashimoto's, which is why Betty got into medicine in the first place. But she and Liv seem to have escaped the curse so far. When it comes to diet, she's always telling me to do as she says and not as she does.

"Duh. Today's Thirsty Thursday. We need cocktails to quench ourselves after all this hotness." Liv gestures toward the magazines, which I now notice are all back copies of PEOPLE's Sexiest Man Alive issues.

"Riiiight." I bob my head in understanding. Betty decided to make each day Liv's home this summer a holiday with a different theme. She's even taking a couple weeks off work, which she never does.

"Don't you dare judge us, missy." Betty takes a spoonful of cookie crumbs. "It is essential to get a little tipsy to properly judge which Hollywood hunk has the best abs. Which reminds me, I have a six-pack of sparkling water in the fridge for you."

Water may not be quite as exciting as a cocktail, but it means I won't spend another sleepless night dealing with a flare-up, so I'll take it. "You're the real MVP, Betty."

I'm about to go grab a water when Liv says, "And speaking of hunks..."

I follow her gaze out the bay window. A beat-up Chevy truck I know all too well is pulling into the driveway, Ty Rossi behind the steering wheel.

"Nooooo," I moan, sinking back down on the chair.

"I know, right?" Betty says, sounding way too entertained by all this. "I haven't had time to make that popcorn yet."

Chapter 5

I crack the front door open, expecting to see Ty's cocky grin. But my view is blocked by what has to be the most enormous binder the world's ever seen.

"Wow." I tilt my head to the side, studying the monstrosity. It's a foot wide and almost as thick. "I know you owe me an apology, but I didn't expect it to be quite so long."

"I'm sorry." Ty lowers the binder enough for me to see the sardonic glint in his eyes. "Who pushed who in the pool again?"

"Ooh, you were so close there. Should've quit while you were ahead."

"It's a thousand degrees out here, and this thing isn't exactly light. Are you gonna make me stand out here all day?"

The sun's at just the right angle, reflecting off the concrete of the porch. I can feel the heat radiating even from inside the doorway. Ty's probably melting. Good.

I shrug. "The pool's nice and cold. I'd be happy to push you in again."

"Hi, Ty." The hardwood floor lets out a creak as Betty comes up beside me. "What a pleasant surprise." Her eyes flick to mine like she's telepathically chastising me for being rude. "Why don't you come on in?" She reaches around me and swings the door open.

"You know what they say about inviting evil spirits into your house," I mutter.

"Thanks, Betty. I'd love to." Ty's expression is gloating. His arm brushes against mine as he follows Betty into the kitchen, and I wish I could erase my body's visceral memories of him. Goosebumps erupt on my skin despite the heat flooding through the open door. I can't help thinking about how it used to feel to be wrapped up in those arms.

I thunk my forehead against the door as I push it shut. I need a field guide for dealing with my ex-boyfriend. I want to hate him, but I also remember loving him, and the line between those two emotions is maddeningly blurry.

"Quinn, how about that water?" Betty's voice comes from the kitchen.

"Yes, please," I call and turn to follow after them.

Ty's at the counter-height table in the breakfast nook. The binder's open before him, and he's flicking through the pages.

This is fine. My ex-boyfriend is sitting in the kitchen like he still belongs here, which is fine. I'm fine. Toooooootally fine. I just need someone to pass that message along to my heart. It's doing a complicated tap routine against my sternum, attempting to channel Fred Astaire.

"So, are you penning the next great American novel or what?" Liv asks, nodding toward the binder. She's standing in front of the marble countertop, shaking a cocktail mixer. Sunshine glints off the rows of white subway tiles that line the wall behind her. Betty pulls a couple of bottles of sparkling water out of the fridge and sets them on the table. I don't miss the fact that she places mine right next to Ty's.

Betty's always liked him. She tried to convince me to go talk to him after we broke up, but I couldn't. I was too angry. And since everything that happened between us was entirely his fault, I wasn't about to go crawling back to him. I kept expecting him to turn up on our doorstep with an apology and a handful of sunflowers. I waited all summer, but he never showed.

I scoop up the bottle of water in stride and stomp to the other side of the table.

"I'm just dropping off Quinn's homework." Ty flips the binder shut and pats the cover.

I do my best imitation of Liv's eyebrow quirk. "What are you talking about?"

"This is Paula's Founders Festival binder with all the event details."

"You're joking." A lead weight settles in my gut as I examine the sheer enormity of the binder. It's going to take me forever to read through that thing. I groan and let my head thump forward against the table. At this rate, I'm going to give myself a concussion by the time Ty leaves the house.

"And you have Paula's Texas-sized binder because?" Liv plops down in the chair next to mine and sips her margarita.

"Quinn and I are running the festival while Paula's out of town." Ty smiles at me in a way I can only describe as antagonistic. I stick my tongue out at him because that is the level of maturity I've achieved this week.

"The two of you are running the festival?" Betty's eyebrows practically touch her hairline as she glances back and forth between Ty and me. "Together?"

"Paula's mom broke her hip," I explain. "She had to go stay with her and left us in charge."

"Is her mom okay?" Betty asks.

"Yeah. Paula called Giselle while I was at the school. She said her mom will be fine, but she'll have to stay with her until she's back on her feet again."

"And Paula thought leaving you two in charge was safe?" Liv asks, a spark of amusement dancing in her eyes.

"As long as no one stands too close to any open water, we should be alright," Ty says.

I roll my eyes. "Oh, get over it."

Betty doesn't even bother to hide her smile. "Have I mentioned popcorn? Liv, baby, we'll have to run to the market and stock up. Whatever we have in the pantry, it isn't going to be enough."

I make a mental note to short-sheet her bed later.

"Speaking of popcorn," Ty says, scooting the binder toward me. "The first item on our to-do list is to pick a film for the last night of the festival. We're doing a movie in the park."

"I'm aware of that. Unlike some people, I actually live here, remember? I've seen the itinerary on all the flyers around town." I start turning the—I kid you not—thousands of pages in the binder.

"Oh, that's right." The sarcasm in Ty's voice is thick. "You moved here—what was it? Six years ago now? You must know way more than someone who's lived here since they were born."

"Someone who used to live here. Past tense."

Liv slurps her cocktail. I glance over at her and Betty. They're holding their drinks, watching the two of us like this is the most fun they've had all week.

I edit my mental note. I'll be short-sheeting both of their beds later.

"So, what are the movie options anyway?" I ask.

"Please refer to Appendix A, Section 3.5 of the binder," Ty says.

"Why am I not surprised this thing has appendices?" I grumble.

"We've got exactly three hundred and forty-seven titles to choose from. My vote's for The Bourne Identity."

I scoff. "This isn't movie night with your boys. The film is for the whole town. The Bourne Identity is not family-friendly."

"It's PG-13." Ty reaches over and opens the binder to the movie section. "And it's on Paula's list." He jabs a finger at a thumbnail of the movie poster.

"Yeah, I'm gonna go with no."

Ty tosses his hands in the air. "Of course you are. You're going to veto anything I pick."

"Only if you insist on choosing dude-bro flicks."

"Uh-huh. And what would you choose then?" Ty leans back in his chair, folding his arms over his chest.

"Something actually good."

"Be my guest." Ty makes a sweeping gesture toward the binder.

"Fine." I pull it closer, skimming the selections. There are so many movies listed here it's overwhelming. Betty and Liv crowd around me, checking out the titles over my shoulders.

"Drag Me to Hell?" Betty points from behind me. "Sounds promising, but are you sure Paula approved all of these?"

Ty shrugs. "She said to choose something from the list."

I turn the page and find my favorite movie of all time. "Alright, done." I brush my palms against each other. "That was easy. What's next on the to-do list?"

Ty leans forward, peering at the paper. He sees the movie I'm looking at and groans, sinking back in his chair. "We're not watching Ever After. No way."

"Excuse you," Liv says, "Ever After happens to be the greatest film in cinematic history."

"The first five hundred times you've watched it, maybe. You all used to torture me with that stupid movie."

Betty gasps and covers Drew Barrymore's ear with a fingertip. "Don't listen to him, Drew. He doesn't mean it."

"With all due respect," Ty holds up his hands, "more people in Rosedale will want to watch The Bourne Identity."

"That's not even kind of true. Way more people are going to want Ever After," I say.

"You seriously think that?"

"I know that."

"Alright, that's simple enough to prove." Ty shoots me that smug smirk of his. "We'll take a poll."

"How? You want to go around and ask every person in Rosedale if they'd rather watch Ever After or," I scrunch up my nose, "The Bourne Identity?"

"Exactly," Ty says like it's no big.

"How would we even do that?"

Ty walks around the table and starts flipping pages again. It takes all my self-control not to scoot my chair away from him. "Section 7F includes a list of every resident in town. They're all going to be at the festival. We can have them write down their votes throughout the week. Whichever movie gets the most wins."

"Oh, yeah." Betty sits down. "That sounds way easier than compromising on a film you both like."

Liv snorts. "It is for them."

"What do you say?" Ty holds his hand out to me. "Do we have a deal? Or are you afraid you'll have to admit I know this town better than you do?"

"You wish, California Boy." I stand so I'm closer to Ty's eye level. "Let's do this." I take his hand and give it a firm shake. I really, really hate that I remember every single callus on his fingers.

Chapter 6

- -

I log into Zoom and adjust my laptop screen so my face is centered. I have a standing, bi-weekly appointment with Janet, my course advisor, to review my progress. I just wish I had more to report.

Drumming my thumbs against my denim cut-offs, I wait for Janet to join the meeting. My eyes land on the festival binder, taking up most of the countertop next to me. I scowl at it. I was going to spend last night studying for an exam in my Current Issues in Nutrition class. Instead, I read every single page of that stupid binder. The idea of Ty knowing more than I do about what we're supposed to be doing for the kickoff tomorrow was unbearable. I stayed up until two in the morning, reading.

I tug at the t-shirt sticking to my skin. It's uncomfortably hot again today. I hop off the barstool in my little kitchen and flip on the ceiling fan. Betty may not charge me for the utilities in this place, but I make sure allowing me to live here costs her as little as possible. I only turn on the AC when I absolutely need to. My flip-flops slap against the gray stone tile as I walk over to the windows that line the back wall and overlook the pool. I push them open, trying to get some air flowing.

As soon as I sit back down, my computer lights up with Janet's perpetually smiling face. "Hello, Quinn Kelley! How are we doing today?" Janet is always super upbeat. I have suspicions she's powered by nothing but rainbows and puppy cuddles.

"Hey, Janet," I say. "Doing good. How are you?"

"Every day is what you make it. So I'm wonderful." Janet has a tendency to speak in motivational quotes. It's annoying but oddly inspirational. "Let's talk about you," she continues. "Are you ready for your Current Issues exam?"

I sigh, fiddling with the ends of my ponytail. "Not exactly."

"Oh." Janet blinks in surprise. This is the first time I've ever been behind on an assignment. Ever. Thanks a lot, Ty Rossi. "Well, have you started working on the unit?"

"Yes. I've done all the reading. But, something just...came up. One of my friends had to help a sick relative, and she asked me to assist with some events happening here in town this week."

"Well, slow progress is better than no progress." Janet's smile is so bright it's like her teeth are made out of glitter. "And it's always important to give back to our communities. What if we reschedule your test for the following Friday? That way, you can focus on your events before you have to hit the books again. Will that work?"

"That's great. Thanks, Janet. I promise I'll be prepared." I decide not to tell Janet that my helping with the festival has as much to do with wanting to outshine Ty as it does with giving back to my community.

"Well, don't worry about things you can't control. You didn't choose for this to happen, and I am confident you'll nail the exam.

Besides, you've still got plenty of time to complete your certification before the summer's over."

A grin spreads over my face. Becoming a certified nutrition counselor may not be as impressive to some people as a college degree, but I've worked hard for this. Just because my dad works at a marketing firm doesn't mean he makes a ton of money. When he can afford to help me, I have to put the money toward prescription costs. I've paid for my tuition myself, and I've aced every test.

It's crucial that I know what I'm talking about when I graduate. Taking on a career as a counselor means people will be relying on me, and I take the responsibility seriously. I never want my clients to struggle like I did while we were trying to figure out all the kinks in my own diet.

"I'm so glad you had time to fit me into your busy schedule this week because I have something I think you'll be interested to hear about." Janet claps her hands together excitedly.

"What's that?" I laugh. Janet is very extra, but her enthusiasm is contagious. I always feel at least sixty-three percent happier after talking to her.

"I'm sending you an email," Janet says, clicking at her keyboard.

My laptop pings with a notification. I click over to my inbox and read the subject line—'Application for Happy Spoons Grant.'

My forehead scrunches. "What's a Happy Spoons Grant?"

"I'm so glad you asked," Janet chirps. "Every year, the Happy Spoons Grant is awarded to one graduating student planning to use their nutrition certification to help people with chronic illnesses."

Ah, the name makes sense. People with health issues like mine call themselves spoonies. It's a reference to a lupus blogger named Christine Miserandino, who explained the lack of energy most of us experience using spoons. The idea is that you start the day with a handful of metaphorical spoons. Everything you do takes up a certain number of your spoons, so you have to plan your day to avoid running out.

"The grant's for ten thousand dollars," Janet says. "And I think you'd be an excellent fit."

My mouth drops open. Ten thousand dollars is a lot of money. I could easily launch my business with that kind of cash. It's more than enough to pay for the licenses and insurance I'll need. I could even self-publish the cookbook of autoimmune protocol treats I've been secretly daydreaming about.

"I don't know what to say." I blink at the computer. "That sounds like such a great opportunity."

"Well, why not be the girl who decided to go for it then? It can't hurt to try."

I bite my lip. Janet would think I had a chance at getting this grant no matter how slim the odds were because, well, that's Janet. It's hard for me to muster that kind of optimism, but she has a point. "What would I need to do?"

"Just turn in the application before the deadline next Wednesday. You'll definitely want to include some examples to demonstrate how you're implementing what you've learned to make a difference in the lives of people with chronic conditions."

"I post my AIP recipes on Instagram," I say. I share recipes and cooking tips that comply with the autoimmune protocol diet, which most people with serious chronic illnesses have to follow. I create recipes for delicious baked treats that allow people to eliminate foods from their diets that cause flare-ups. I put a ton of work into those recipes because baked goods were what I missed most when

I first started the diet. Figuring out how to replace ingredients I reacted to has taken me years to master, and I love sharing what I've learned with others.

"That's amazing," Janet says. I'm sure plenty of people find your posts incredibly helpful. The judges for the grant do usually like to see some real-world examples, though. You teach baking classes in your town, right?"

"I do, but my classes don't exactly draw a big crowd here in Rosedale." My class this morning had a whopping one attendee, Jenny Jenkins. And she only came because she thought the word Paleo meant white chocolate. Tapping my fingers against the counter, I try to think of an example of how I'm helping people IRL and come up empty.

"Well, two heads are always better than one. Let's brainstorm. What about those events you're participating in this week?" Janet asks. "Is there a way you can incorporate an activity that could improve the wellness of your community?"

I frown. There isn't a way to work dealing with dietary restrictions into the karaoke night, kickball game, or rain gutter regatta. Especially with how competitive the people of Rosedale get at those things.

"We're having a bake sale?" I say like it's a question. "I could bake batches of AIP and regular cookies and have a contest to see if people can guess which is which. Maybe I could convince people you don't need added sugar to make food taste good."

I'm already getting excited about the idea. It would be fun, and my carob chip cookies are incredible if I say so myself.

Janet starts to nod, but then her eyes flick to the corner of the screen. She freezes. I've never seen Janet look unenthusiastic about, well, anything. She must think the bake sale is a terrible idea, which surprises me. It might not be ground-breaking, but I didn't think it was that bad.

"Or I could come up with something else?" I ask, confused.

"No, no. The bake sale would be perfect," Janet says, still looking rattled. Her eyes keep darting to the side, and her eternal smile has vanished. "It's just, uh," Janet drops her voice to a whisper, "why is that man in your backyard green?"

"What?" I swivel around on my barstool to look out the windows. Sure enough, standing beside the pool is our next-door neighbor, Gary Andrews. He's wearing a pair of pineapple-patterned swim trunks, and his skin is as green as grass from the tip of his head to his calves. He has on white socks with his sandals, so I can't see his toes, but I'm guessing they're Hulk-colored too. What I can't guess at is why.

I turn back to Janet. "Um, I should probably go."

"That seems like a good idea." Janet recovers some of her usual effervescence. "Keep me posted on your application, though. And remember, always choose joy."

"Right. You too, Janet." I flip the lid of my laptop shut and hustle to the door. This week just keeps getting weirder and weirder.

Chapter 7

"**G**ary, what is even happening right now?" I almost trip over my flip-flops as I rush across the patio to where he's laying an oversized beach towel across a lawn chair. Heat radiates off the concrete, making sweat bead across my hairline.

Gary tilts his head to the side, staring at me like he has no idea what I'm talking about. Someone in the neighborhood fires up a lawnmower. The ch, ch, ch of a sprinkler comes from next door.

"Betty told me I could use the pool whenever I wanted," he says. "If this is a bad time, though, I can come back later."

I'm at a loss for what to say. Gary's typically near-translucent skin is green. He's always oblivious, especially considering he's in charge of the neighborhood watch. Gary's the kind of guy who wears sweater vests and khaki cargo shorts year-round. And he's been rocking black-framed glasses since way before they were cool, and I'm sure he'll continue to do so long afterward.

"It's not that. You can swim if you want to. But..." I make a sweeping motion, gesturing at his skin. "Gary, why are you green?"

"Oh, is that what you're on about?" Gary chuckles like I'm being mellow-dramatic. "It's sunscreen, obviously."

"Sunscreen?" I blink at him. Who would willingly buy sunblock that turns them into the Jolly Green Giant? I mean, I know this is Gary we're talking about, but come on.

"I'm surprised you haven't heard of it. It's the latest thing." Gary plants his hands on his hips, making his moss-colored belly protrude. Since his hair looks like it was styled using a Flowbee, I doubt he's in the know on current trends.

"You should really consider picking some up," Gary continues. "It makes it so you can see every spot you miss while lathering up. You can never be too careful. Thousands of people die every year from melanoma, you know." He blinks. Even his eyelids are a brilliant shade of emerald.

"Well, you've certainly got yourself covered."

Gary's got a reputation for being a hypochondriac. Not that I'm one to judge. I was convinced I had just about every terminal illness in existence when we were trying to figure out what was making me sick. But Gary took it to a new level last year when he had a stomach ache and started telling the whole town he had PCOS. Betty had to explain to him that only people with ovaries can get polycystic ovary syndrome.

"If you do decide to pick some up, talk to that young man of yours. He helped me find this. Isn't it fun?" Gary holds his arms out like he's Edward freaking Cullen, walking into a sunny meadow. But I'm barely paying attention because this situation suddenly makes a lot more sense. I can't believe I didn't realize it before. Gary transforming into Gamora's twin the week Ty happens to come back to town couldn't be a coincidence.

I breathe in the smell of freshly mown grass and try to keep a handle on the irritation flickering through me. "When you say, 'that young man,' do you mean Ty?"

"Of course. Mr. Rossi and his two friends came up to me when I was in Winchester's, perusing the sunblock. I was going to go with my usual SPF 100, but he stopped me in the nick of time. He said he got this one off the special shelves in back." Gary grabs a bottle of sunscreen out of his beach bag and hands it to me. "It was the same price as all the other brands but with double the protection. Talk about a no-brainer."

I read the label, turning the bottle over in my hands. "Gary, this doesn't say anything about the lotion turning your skin green. Didn't that seem a little suspicious to you?"

Gary scoffs. "Well, they can't make it too obvious. Otherwise, everyone would be buying it. They'd sell out."

I hand the sunscreen back to him. "I may not be a business guru, but isn't selling a product everybody wants kind of the goal?"

"Young lady," Gary laughs, "you clearly know nothing about running a business. Selling out of your product isn't a good thing. It's all about supply and demand."

I wasn't aware someone could sound so ridiculous and condescending at the same time, but Gary knocked it out of the park. The term 'mansplainer' flashes in my mind in big, neon letters.

"Well, you just got punked. That is regular ole sunblock three idiots put dye in. Have fun washing it off."

"Dye? Don't be absurd." Gary gives me a patronizing pat on the arm.

"Alrighty then." I spin around on my heel and stomp back toward the pool house. "Enjoy your swim, Gary." I toss a wave over my shoulder without turning around.

The men in this town are seriously going to be the death of me.

Chapter 8

<hr>

"I'm not complaining, but I'm surprised you agreed to join us for Fine Dining Friday." Liv links her elbow with mine. The worn leather of her black jacket is as soft as velvet against my arm.

"You and me both, sister," I mutter.

There's exactly one restaurant in Rosedale, Rossi's Italian Cuisine. And it's owned by, you guessed it, Ty's family. Usually, I'm all about going to Rossi's. Just because I'm not Ty's number-one fan anymore doesn't mean I don't still love his family. I'm convinced his dad, Marco, is an actual angel. He goes out of his way to make food I can eat. And he ensures there isn't any cross-contamination that would cause issues for me.

I fully intended to avoid the place until Ty went back to UCLA. But that was before he decided to dye my next-door neighbor green.

"I have words for my festival co-host," I say. "I mean, seriously, are we twelve? What adult person thinks it's funny to turn another human being green? Even if it is Gary."

Liv barks out a laugh, which she tries to hide with a cough. I scowl at her.

"It's a tiny bit funny," she says. Our shoes crunch against the loose pebbles on the sidewalk as we follow Betty through the town square. The trees lining Main Street glow in the white, twinkle lights that adorn them year-round.

"You think you have words for him?" Betty shoots a glance over her shoulder at me. "I'm the one with a green swimming pool, and you better believe it won't be me pumping out all the water and replacing it." She holds the door of the restaurant open. The intoxicating smell of roasted tomatoes and melted cheese wafts through the air.

We walk into the warm light of the foyer. Rossi's is all dark wooden booths and cozy golden lanterns. With the stone flooring and Venetian plaster walls, it has the vibe of an Italian piazza. Or what I would imagine one would be like anyway.

Liv's phone buzzes, and she fishes it from her jacket pocket. She's waiting to find out if she was elected president of her sorority, the Kappa Zetas.

"Any news?" I ask, even though I'm guessing from the slump of her shoulders there isn't.

"No. I'm starting to think they're hazing me again because this is torture."

I give her a side hug as we step up to the hostess stand where Ty's sister Francie is organizing a stack of menus. When she sees us, her flawlessly-painted red lips break into a big smile.

"Quinn! You're here. I didn't think we'd see your cute face while Ty was in town." Francie knows Ty and I didn't end things on a high note, but she still treats me like part of the family. "So, how are the Kelley gals tonight?"

My mom and Betty were adamant about passing the Kelley surname down to their daughters. They believed women have as much right to carry on their family name as men do. Betty's never been married, but Mom insisted on keeping her name when she tied the knot.

"We're good. Annoyed, but good." I scan the dining room, searching for Ty. I see his other sisters, Lisa and Gianna, taking orders, but no sign of that over-inflated head of his. Ty's sisters are just as gorgeous as he is, with their shiny, dark hair and olive complexions.

"I've got a bone to pick with that brother of yours," I tell Francie.

"Speaking of bones to pick." Betty brushes past us, striding over to Kelvin and Chance. They're hunched over a red-and-white-checked table, laughing as they sneak glances at Gary. He's sitting next to the window, examining one of the laminated menus through his thick-framed glasses and looking distinctly green.

"Tell me he didn't." Francie purses her ruby lips, glancing from Gary back to Chance and Kelvin and connecting the dots that lead straight to her older brother.

"Oooh, he did." Liv plucks one of the menus from Francie's hands and starts perusing the dessert section.

Francie shakes her head. "Mama is going to murder that boy."

"Only if I don't get to him first," I say, watching Betty bend down and plant her palms on Chance and Kelvin's table.

"Hi, guys," she says. "I hope you didn't have plans for the rest of the weekend because guess who's draining and refilling a sixteen-thousand-gallon pool that mysteriously turned green this afternoon?"

I can only see the back of Chance's head from here, but his pale ears turn bright red. If we didn't already know they were responsible for Gary's dye job, those ears alone would be a dead giveaway.

Kelvin, on the other hand, is still smiling. To be fair, I've never seen Kelvin without a smile on his face. He's one of those people who are perpetually happy. Having a good time is Kelvin's M.O. With his dark skin and swoon-inducing dimples, he's an attractive guy. Too bad he's got the maturity level of a thirteen-year-old. As do Chance and Ty.

"Sorry, Betty," Kelvin says, flashing her a grin that could charm the habit off of a freaking nun.

"Yeah, me too," Betty says, voice dripping with false sincerity. "I'll see you and your third musketeer at seven tomorrow morning. And bring a towel. You're going to need it."

"But I—" Kelvin starts, but Betty cuts him off.

"Kelvin Jones, do not make me call your grandmother."

"Yes, ma'am," he says, staring at the tablecloth.

"We'll be there," Chance adds, sounding a little too eager. He's always been a suck-up, especially for a guy who's pranked every person in this town at one point or another.

"Alright, then." Betty whirls on her heel to face us and mouths the word 'boys.'

I agree with the sentiment, but I know exactly which boy was the brains behind this scheme, and he isn't sitting in the dining room.

I turn to Francie. "Where is he?"

"In the kitchen. Go ahead." She tilts her head toward the back of the restaurant. "Let's get you a table," she says to Liv and Betty.

They follow her as I cut a path through the tables that glow in the candlelight. The smell of freshly baked bread makes my mouth water. I can't remember the last time I ate them, but my tastebuds will never forget Marco's bread bites, light and airy with gooey garlic butter. Eating one would almost be worth the inevitable flare-up the gluten would cause.

I push the swinging, stainless steel door to the kitchen a little too hard. It bangs against the wall, making a few of the cooks jump and glance up from the simmering pots that litter the stovetops. The air is heavy with the scent of basil and pesto.

"Quinn!" Marco Rossi walks away from the row of immaculate white plates he's inspecting on the counter to give me a hug. "Are you here to place an order or to see your favorite old man?"

I laugh, hugging Marco back. He is truly one of the greatest humans on the planet. "Both."

"You want the gluten-free meatballs with a side of asparagus?" Marco's eyes crinkle. They're the same shade of brown as Ty's. They emanate warmth and comfort, like melted chocolate. The gray hair at his temples has settled in over the last few years, only making him more charming.

"That would be perfect." I give Marco's hand a grateful squeeze. "I have to admit, I'm here to yell at your son, though. Is he here?"

"Aaaah." Marco bobs his head in understanding. "No doubt, he has it coming."

"He does." I look past Marco's shoulder and see Ty standing next to the double-stacked commercial ovens.

He folds his arms over his chest, walking toward me. "Conspiring against me with my own father. This is a new low."

"And tricking Gary into using sunscreen that dyed his skin green is what? A personal best for you?"

"You dyed Gary green?" Marco's eyes are wide as he looks at his son. I don't miss the spark of amusement there and try not to roll my eyes.

"I can neither confirm nor deny these ludicrous allegations." Ty grins, looking entirely too pleased with himself.

"It isn't funny." I toss my hands in the air, exasperated. "What if he'd been allergic to the dye? I doubt you bothered checking before you tried to one-up Ashton Kutcher."

Ty's expression shifts from self-satisfied to contrite. His eyes drop to the immaculate tile floor, hand scrubbing at the back of his neck. "You're right. I didn't bother checking. I should have."

His gaze blinks back up, colliding with mine, and I can tell he isn't thinking about Gary and his potential allergies but mine. We were together long enough for Ty to have witnessed my body's bizarre reactions to the most innocuous things. The way he's biting his lips together. The flat, sad expression in his eyes. It makes me believe that he genuinely understands why his latest prank is triggering for me. But seeing that understanding makes my heart constrict painfully inside my chest. Where was that understanding when I needed it three years ago? And why can't he actually stop and think about the potential fallout of his actions before he pulls these ludicrous pranks?

My lips part. There are so many things I want to say, but I don't know where to begin.

"I'm just going to leave you two to it." Marco pats me on the shoulder before returning to his pasta.

I don't blame him for exiting stage left. I'd like to do the same. Ty and I had so many arguments over his pranking hobby when we were together, and Marco has certainly heard it all before. I thought time healed all wounds. But it's as if we picked right up where we left off three years ago when Ty skipped town without a goodbye.

"It was a joke, Quinn." Ty's eyes travel over my face, studying me like he's watching for signs of an impending explosion. "I should have been more careful, but Gary is perfectly fine. There's no reason to be this upset...again."

I can feel my chest turning hot and blotchy and try to cover it with a hand. But the way he said 'again' is infuriating, like I'm some hysterical woman who is always flying off the handle for no reason. I want him to take accountability for his actions. Not downplay them to make me seem like the one who's out of line.

"Well, since your last prank got me arrested, I guess this is a bit of a hot-button for me. I'm sure you can understand." I'm fighting to keep my voice calm, even, but my words echo through the now-silent kitchen. The cooks are hanging off our every word. I've been bottling up these feelings for years now, though. I can't hold them inside a second longer.

When I moved to Rosedale, I was immediately charmed by Ty. He was always laughing and having a good time. Being around him was a distraction from all the health nonsense I was dealing with. He made me happy. By the end of our senior year, though, some of the appeal of dating the class clown began to wear off.

We were always fighting about how I thought he needed to grow up and take things more seriously. He insisted I should learn how to relax and have fun. I spent weeks asking him not to, but he went ahead with the elaborate senior prank he planned with Chance and Kelvin. They captured hundreds of live bats and set them loose in the school. Unfortunately, the dummies didn't notice they'd left the keys they stole from the janitor in the lock outside the door before shutting themselves in the gymnasium.

Ty called and asked me to come let them out, and like a moron, I went. I unlocked the door at almost the exact moment the police arrived. All four of us were arrested. Even though I had nothing to do with the bats, I was still illegally on the premises, so I got charged with trespassing and sentenced to sixty hours of community service. Ty and I got into a huge fight in the parking lot of the police station. It makes my heart ache even now to think about the words we screamed at each other that we can never take back.

To top it all off, animal control was concerned the bats could be carrying rabies, so the school had to shut down for a week while they trapped them all. There were a lot of meetings between everyone's parents and the school administration. They finally agreed to let us complete our finals virtually instead of making us repeat our last semester of classes.

To say my dad wasn't happy would be an understatement. He threatened to make me move home, which was not only the last thing I wanted; it would have risked my health. Betty eventually convinced him my condition—which we'd just gotten under control at the time—was the most important thing to consider. He caved and allowed me to stay in Rosedale, but with the stipulation that if I put another toe out of line, I'd be on a plane back to New York. I spent that entire summer waiting for Ty to show up on my doorstep with an apology, but it never came. It's been three years of radio silence until he showed up again this week.

Ty takes a step closer to me. He lowers his voice so no one can overhear him. "Quinn, seriously, how long are you going to be mad at me?"

I shoot a glance around the kitchen. Everyone is working really hard to make it look like they aren't paying attention to us.

"I'm starting to feel like a broken record," I say, "but probably until you actually apologize."

"I am sorry. Truly. I am." There's so much sincerity in his eyes; it makes me physically ache. Part of me wants to believe him. Despite everything that happened, I miss him. I miss us. But another part of me is holding onto the hurt and anger like a life preserver because keeping Ty at a distance is safe. He can't hurt me again if I don't let him get close.

"It was a stupid prank," Ty continues. "You told me not to go through with it, and I should've listened. You have no idea how much I regret that. Is there any way we can leave it in the past and move forward? Please?"

I blow out a breath, puffing out my lips. Despite his genuineness, his apology feels lacking. Because it's not just the prank I'm upset about. It isn't even that I got arrested for something he did. It's the fact that he left without looking back or showing any concern for the consequences his actions cost me. But it isn't like I can tell him his apology isn't good enough, then I'd be the one to look like a complete jerk.

And while I might not be ready to totally forgive him, I also recognize that we have to spend the next week working together. I can't let our issues impact the Founder's Festival that Paula put so much time and care into planning.

I squeeze my eyes shut, forcing down the storm of emotions thrumming through my system. "Okay," I finally say.

"Yeah?" Ty's brows lift hopefully.

I bounce my shoulders in a shrug, acting as if I couldn't care less. "Yeah. Let's move forward."

Ty's face breaks into a smile, and dang it if that stupid smile doesn't still have the power to make me melt like an Otter Pop at a Fourth of July parade.

"Cool. I'll see you at the bonfire tomorrow," he says.

"Oh, I'll see you before then. Gary went swimming in Betty's pool and turned the water green. She's expecting you and your little entourage to be at our house at seven in the morning to fix it. Should be fun."

Ty's smile falters. And yeah, sometimes I really love karma.

"Have a great night," I call over my shoulder and stride out of the kitchen.

Chapter 9

The patio table is cluttered with the Founder's Festival binder, my laptop, and the stacks of Liv and Betty's mass-market romance novels. They've declared today Smut-a-thon Saturday. They're perusing the descriptions on the back of the books while I edit my latest photos for the Gram.

The air above the concrete is hazy from the heat, but Betty's oversized beach umbrella blocks out the worst of the sun's death rays. I pour a glass of the pink lemonade I made using lemon juice, frozen strawberries, and coconut cream. It's tart and completely delicious, if I do say so myself.

"I know this one sounds a little out there, but I'm pretty sure my life won't be complete until I've read Ravished by Raptors." Betty holds out a book with a flourish.

My jaw almost hits the table. A woman in a black bikini lounges across the cover like one of Jack Dawson's French girls with—no joke—a velociraptor standing behind her.

"That is not a real book." Liv grabs the novel from Betty and starts rifling through the pages. "I'm not usually one to judge another person for their kink, but this is out there even for you."

"I'm not sure what you're implying, daughter of mine," Betty snatches the book back, "but dinosaur erotica is a whole thing. Ask Google."

"I am definitely not Googling that."

"Did you just say dinosaur erotica?" Ty squints over at us, scrunching his nose. He's bent over, hooking a hose to the swimming pool pump. He rubs a hand across his forehead, which is shiny with sweat, making his inky hair curl.

He spent the entire morning measuring the chemical levels with Kelvin and Chance. They had to use Sodium Thiosulfate to reduce the chlorine and make it safe to drain. Their hands have all turned a spectacular shade of green, which makes me feel all warm and fuzzy every time I look at them.

"This is an A and B conversation, mister," Betty calls. "So I suggest you C your way out of it. Also, you boys should grab some water. I don't need anyone dehydrating on my watch."

Ty yells for Chance and Kelvin to come and take a break. They're out in the field behind the pool house, where they've drug the other end of the hose. They drop it in the long grass and trudge back to the patio.

It's very cathartic, sitting here, drinking lemonade, while the three of them pay the consequences for their boneheaded actions. The universe is finally balancing the scales after what they put me through in high school.

Not that the day's been all sunshine and revenge over here. I've been trying and failing to make progress on my application for the grant. The bake sale is my best and only idea to demonstrate how I'm using my nutrition certification to make a difference in anyone's life. I switched to editing photos to try and get my creative juices flowing.

I turn my attention back to Photoshop. Giselle took a picture of me baking Paleo brownies the other day. I'm painstakingly removing any trace of the dark circles from beneath my eyes.

"What are you doing?" Ty says from right behind my shoulder, making me jump. My hand knocks into my lemonade. It teeters dangerously close to my keyboard. Ty catches it just in time.

"Do you know what boundaries are?" I turn in my chair to scowl up at him. "I'm editing a picture. What does it look like I'm doing?"

Betty tosses Ty a bottle of water. He unscrews the cap, chugging it and scrubbing the back of his green hand across his lips. I'm more than a little disappointed when it doesn't leave a slime-colored smudge.

"I'm sorry," he says. "I don't understand why you'd want to Photoshop your face. It doesn't need any editing. It's...fine."

"Wow. That was almost sweet there, Rossi," Liv says without looking up from the book she's reading titled, Sex and the Single Vampire.

"For real, though." Chance wipes at the sweat sticking his red hair to his forehead. "Why do girls always have to FaceTune their pictures before they post them?"

There's a loaded moment where the only sound is the sucking of the pump, siphoning the water out of the pool.

Liv side-eyes Chance. "I assume you're looking for reasons outside of the ridiculous and unattainable beauty standards society places on women?"

"Ummmm..." Chance's face, already flushed from the heat, turns bright pink.

"Abort. Abort. Activate emergency foot-in-mouth protocol." Kelvin nudges Chance in the ribs.

"If you must know, some of us can't control the fact that we get dark circles under our eyes," I say. "But we can control whether or not the thousands of strangers who follow us on Instagram get to see them."

Ty scoffs. "Literally, no one cares."

"Hi. Have you met the internet? Everyone cares." I shut my laptop, so he can't see the screen.

"You do know you can't control what everyone thinks of you, right?" Ty frowns.

Leave it to Ty to cut straight through my carefully constructed facade and get to the heart of the matter. Of course, he'd realize my Photoshop obsession comes from my need to control how other people see me. I really hate that he knows me better than anyone else, including Betty and Liv.

He'll never understand what it feels like to be completely out of control, though. To have some mysterious sickness you can't figure out. He can never know how once you get that control back, you'll do everything in your power to hang onto it. And apparently, he also doesn't get that running a successful wellness business means I need to be the picture of health constantly. Even if I have to fake it sometimes.

I force my lips into a syrupy smile. "Well, I can certainly try."

"Yeah, that seems healthy." Ty shoots his water bottle into the garbage can like a basketball hoop. Naturally, it goes in. "Let's finish up," he says to Kelvin and Chance. "I want to try and scrub this crap off my hands before the bonfire tonight."

He walks back toward the pool. The white tank top he's wearing with his swim trunks shows off his toned arms. His sweaty skin glistens in the sunlight, and my gaze lingers on his biceps, which instantly annoys me. I mean, really. Who needs muscles like that if they aren't part of a pro-arm-wrestling circuit?

I turn back to the table to see Betty watching me. The corners of her mouth are bent in a worried expression I haven't seen in a while.

"What's the matter?" I ask, taking a drink of my lemonade.

"Okay, don't get mad." She leans forward, resting her arms on a pile of romance novels.

"What a totally comforting way to begin a conversation." I slump back in my chair, waiting to see where she's going with this.

"It's just that Ty has a point about not being able to control everything all the time, kid. Between your mom and your health, you've been dealt some really shitty hands. I get that you don't want to repeat those experiences. But the thing about life is that there will always be stuff that's out of your control. And sometimes the greatest things that happen to us are things we never planned for." She glances over at Liv.

"Yeah, yeah. Living, breathing accident over here." Liv waves a hand, but she's smirking.

"Happy accident," Betty corrects.

"You sound like Janet," I mumble. I understand what Betty's saying, but I'll do anything to keep my life from spiraling away from me again. I can't imagine a scarier feeling than that.

"Well, Janet sounds like one cool cat." The look Betty gives me is so earnest I can't be annoyed with her. "Alright, overprotective aunt spiel over. Put that laptop away, because I've got a passage to share with you." She holds up a copy of Date Me, Baby, One More Time and waggles her eyebrows.

I laugh. "Okay, but make it quick. I've only got," I check my watch, "fifteen minutes before I have to get ready for the bonfire."

"That's what she said." Liv steals a sip of my lemonade and flips the page of her vampire book.

Chapter 10

My hands shake, and I'm positive my chest is covered in angry, red splotches. I stare at the microphone stand set up inside the gazebo. I've read the bonfire night section of that stupid binder at least twenty times, and nowhere did it mention that I'd have to give a Founder's Festival kickoff speech. Nowhere.

Most people would expect someone who teaches for a living to be more comfortable with public speaking. But since I've only had at most five people in my classroom at a time—two of whom were Liv and Betty—I don't have much experience.

A pair of cymbals crash as the marching band launches into the Rosedale High fight song, and I just about jump out of my skin. Some poor soul wearing the Larry the Liger costume does a tumbling pass in front of the giant woodpile Ty, Chance, and Kelvin erected. The crowd erupts in applause, and someone starts chanting fi-re, fi-re, fi-re, dragging the word out into two syllables. Within seconds, the rest of the town has joined in. My heart pounds faster as the chant gains momentum.

A broad hand closes around my shoulder, and I gasp. Having someone grab me unexpectedly when adrenaline is already thrumming through my system has the unfortunate side effect of making me lash out. Literally. My elbow shoots back in a gut punch entirely of its own accord—a move I learned in a self-defense class Betty made Liv and I take back in high school. I feel it collide with a set of washboard abs.

Oomph. The air whooshes out of Ty's lungs, and his stomach contracts. He bends forward at the waist, biting his lips together like he's trying to keep himself from cursing.

"Oops." I bare my teeth in a grimace as I look down at Ty's hunched form. The muscles in his neck are rigid, either from pain or irritation. "You scared me."

"You don't say." Ty straightens, sucking a heavy breath through his nostrils and giving me a death glare. Definitely irritation, then.

"Sorry." I give him an awkward pat on the shoulder.

Ty sighs. "You know, it's almost worth getting gut-checked to hear you apologize for once."

"Oh, haha. You're hilarious."

"So people tell me."

The band switches to "Uptown Funk," and everyone whoops. People begin dancing around the woodpile. Gary busts out his best imitation of the sprinkler, looking utterly ridiculous but distinctly less green than yesterday. This place is like the PBS version of Sodom and Gomorrah.

Ty catches my eye. "So, you okay?"

"I'm...fine." I narrow my eyes at him. Ty being nice is unsettling. Snarky Ty, I can handle. Angry Ty? Bring it on. But considerate Ty? I have no idea what to do with that. I clear my throat. "I'm great.

Perfect." My heart is still beating twice its normal pace. I press my hand over my neck, so he can't see my pulse pounding.

"You sure?" Ty glances from my hand to my eyes. "Because you look like you're about to self-destruct. And if I recall correctly, you aren't a fan of public speaking."

Ty would remember that. He's the one who had to hold my hair back when I was puking from nerves in the classroom garbage can instead of delivering my presentation for our AP Lit class.

"Nope." I give my head a stubborn shake. Admitting I'm on the verge of a meltdown when Ty's all calm and collected is unacceptable. "That whole stage fright thing is ancient history." I wipe my trembling palms against my skinny jeans. "I mean, it would've been wonderful if anywhere in the eleven hundred pages of the binder it had mentioned that we're expected to give a kickoff speech. But I'm totally fine. Cool as a cucumber."

Ty squints at me in the glow of the twinkle lights decorating the gazebo. "Paula has given a kickoff speech before the bonfire for longer than I've been alive. I assumed you knew we'd have to do this." His expression turns gloating. "Since you know this town so well and all."

"Mhmm." I force my lips into a smile even though I'd like to give him another swift elbow to the solar plexus. "Must of slipped my mind while I was busy following up with Giselle about the catering, calling Tom about the wood delivery, and checking in with Chief Johnson to make sure the fire department would be on hand tonight. You know, by myself."

"Well, some of us were cleaning your aunt's swimming pool all day."

"Because some of you decided it was necessary to pull yet another idiotic prank."

"Fi-re! Fi-re! Fi-re! Fi-re!" The crowd picks up their chant again with more enthusiasm than before.

Every drop of blood in my body migrates from my head to my feet. I'm probably paler than Chance. Ty scans my face, and I'm sure he can see my sheer terror. There's no point hiding it. He knows me too well.

"Why don't you just wait here?" Ty asks. "I'll give the speech since you had to work so hard today."

I would sell my left kidney to avoid getting up in front of the entire town. But the sarcasm in Ty's voice makes my hands curl into fists at my sides. There's no freaking way I did all the work this afternoon for him to go up there and take the credit.

"Not a chance, California boy." I reach up and straighten my pristine ponytail, trying to envision myself as Katniss, or Beyonce, or some equally kick-ass female icon. "Let's do this."

"Fine, new girl." Ty looks me up and down like he's sizing me up. "Just try not to puke on me this time."

I scowl at him.

"Fi-re! Fi-re!" The townsfolk are practically screaming now.

"Showtime." Ty holds his hand out to escort me up the gazebo steps. To my complete and utter satisfaction, it's still very green. I smirk as I link my fingers through his and follow him up the stairs. The skin of his palm is warm and rough from spending the day elbow-deep in Betty's pool. I'd never admit it to him, but holding his hand does help calm the butterflies flapping inside my gut.

The audience cheers as we step up to the railing, and the marching band cuts off abruptly, the metallic sound of horns fading into the night.

"Yeah, Quinn!" Liv hollers. Glancing around the park, I spot her and Betty next to the buffet table. Giselle's put out a spread of mini sliders, potato chips, and a variety of pasta salads. Marco is standing under one of the giant maple trees with Ty's sisters. I can't see his mom, Lucia, anywhere, though. Weird. She's usually at all the town events.

Chance and Kelvin are tossing little packets on top of the firewood and dowsing it in kerosene. The chemical sting of it burns my nostrils, and my stomach turns over. I focus on taking deep breaths in through my mouth.

I will not puke. I will not puke. I will not puke.

Ty makes a sweeping gesture toward the mic, murmuring, "Ladies first," against my ear. Goosebumps trail across my skin where his breath kissed it.

"Hello," I say into the mic. It gives a god-awful burst of feedback that screeches through the trees, making everyone wince and sending a flock of birds into the air. I cover my ears as Chance rushes to the speaker and adjusts the dials.

I shift my weight onto my right foot, and my leg trembles like a spoonful of green Jello on the set of Jurassic Park. Crap. My condition occasionally has some fun neurological symptoms, including extreme muscle weakness when I get stressed.

I take a step back, trying to get my muscles under control. My legs wobble, and I wrap my fingers around Ty's arm for balance. He looks down at my shaky legs. His brows draw together in concern, and I can tell he remembers this happening before. He loops his arm around my waist and whispers, "You good?"

I glance out at the thousands of faces staring up at us. "I'm fine," I say, and despite evidence to the contrary, I mean it. Having bizarre symptoms hit you out of nowhere is part of life with a chronic illness. At least this type of episode doesn't make me feel ill or leave me with a splitting headache.

"Do you want me to help you down?"

I meet Ty's eyes. There's no gloating there. No vindictive glint. He's genuinely concerned for my well-being. And darn it, if that doesn't turn my insides to goo.

"I'm alright. Really. Just...don't let me fall?"

Ty's gaze skitters over my face. He nods. "Deal. Let's keep this short and sweet."

"Preaching to the choir, mister."

Chance gives us a thumbs up, and I lean on Ty as we step up to the mic again. I'm surprised it doesn't broadcast the sound of my hammering heartbeat. My arm is draped over Ty's shoulders like we're the best of pals. I catch Betty's eye. Her lips are turned in a frown. She knows exactly what's going on.

"Hello, everyone," Ty says into the microphone. Naturally, it doesn't screech at him. "Welcome to the Rosedale Founder's Festival!" His voice echoes through the park, and everybody cheers like he's Freddie Mercury reincarnated to play a Queen reunion concert.

"Paula wanted us to tell you how sorry she is that she couldn't be here this year," Ty continues. "But Quinn and I will do our best to fill her shoes and make this the finest festival this town's ever seen."

There's another thunderous round of applause. Liv lets out a loud wolf whistle.

"We've got events lined up all week, so be sure to check one of the million flyers hanging around town for the itinerary." Ty looks down at me expectantly, and I blink back at him. He jerks his chin toward the microphone.

"Oh, ummm..." I scramble to think of anything to say. My eyes land on the over-stuffed head of Larry the Liger, and before I can think it through, the words, "Goooo, Ligers!" are out of my mouth, and my fist does a little pump in the air.

Oh. My. God. I am officially never speaking in public again.

The crowd doesn't seem put off by my awkwardness. They cheer, and the marching band strikes up another chorus of the fight song.

Ty and I wave, and he helps me walk down the stairs. Well, he walks. What I'm doing could better be described as vibrating. "Go, Ligers? Are you trying out for the spirit squad?" Ty chuckles.

I really want to pinch him, but since he's currently keeping me from collapsing onto the ground, I resist the temptation.

"I didn't know what else to say." I try to step toward the mountain of firewood where everyone is gathered, but letting go of Ty's arm is a mistake. My legs tremble so hard that you'd think I was standing on a fault line during a quake.

Ty's hands wrap around my waist, holding me steady. He's so close I could press my lips against the skin of his collarbone. I drop my gaze to the ground. His proximity is doing nothing to settle my nerves, which, in turn, is doing nothing to keep my muscles from going haywire.

"Do you want me to carry you home?" Ty has to yell to be heard over the mob. They've started counting down from sixty, like New Year's Eve in Times Square. Kelvin and Chance are standing in the center of the throng, matches in hand. I wonder if I'm the only person who finds that sight extremely disturbing.

"No, I'm fine," I say. "I just need—"

"Step right up. Step right up. I've got your antihistamines right here," Betty calls like a barker selling cotton candy at a baseball game. She and Liv appear next to us. Betty passes me a couple of pills and a bottle of water.

Antihistamines are life savers for me, as is the Cromolyn I take daily—which should be made out of solid gold, considering how much it costs. MCAS is a condition where people's allergen-detecting cells are defective. People with MCAS have mast cells that produce allergic responses to abnormal signals like food and environmental elements. Other things, like stress, can be triggers as well.

I swallow the Zyrtec as Liv grabs my arm and helps me sit on the grass. Ty takes a step back, looking between Betty and me and making sure we've got this handled.

"I know you're, like, a huge Taylor Swift fan and whatever," Liv says. "But I think you might be taking the whole 'Shake it Off' thing a little too literally."

"Yeah, you big drama queen," Betty says. She kneels on the lawn next to me, examining my face closely before turning my arms over to check for hives. "Are we good here?"

I nod. "I feel fine. As soon as these pills kick in, I'll be doing sprints across the park."

"Good thing I wore my running shoes. We'll race." Betty stands up and turns to Ty. "Thanks for giving our girl a hand."

"My pleasure." Ty glances over at me and gives me a close-lipped smile.

"I'm sure it was," Liv mutters, and I scowl at her.

I turn to Ty to thank him myself, but the crowd drowns me out. They shout out the final countdown, "Ten! Nine! Eight! Seven! Six...!"

I take Betty and Liv's hands, and they hoist me to my feet, so I can witness the traditional lighting of the bonfire.

"...Five! Four! Three! Two! One!"

Kelvin and Chance flick their matches on the woodpile, and it ignites in a whoosh. A wall of orange flame leaps into the air, and a cheer rings through the town square. But it's cut off by gasps as the flames transform into flickering shades of green, blue, and purple.

"What kind of sorcery is this?" Gary's voice can be heard above everyone else's oohs and aahs. The leaves in the trees reflect the fire's dancing light, transforming them into a riot of color. It's beautiful and enchanting, and I know exactly which three wizards are responsible.

I turn to Ty, tilting my head to the side and raising my eyebrows.

He shrugs, looking almost sheepish. "They're called magical flames. I thought it would be fun."

I shake my head at him but can't hide the smile creeping across my face. Of course, even literal fire isn't exciting enough for Ty.

Chapter 11

Baking isn't an art. It's a science.

I use an ice cream scoop to measure out cookie dough. I make sure the ratio of dough to carob chips matches the other cookies on the baking sheet exactly. These have to be perfect. Not only are they for the Founder's Festival bake sale this afternoon, but they're also for the Happy Spoons Grant. I need photographic evidence of Rosedale's residents enjoying them to include with my application.

"Those look great, Hun." My dad's face grins out at me from my phone. I propped it up on the counter with my selfie stick, so we can FaceTime while I prep for the bake sale.

Dad's ashy-blond hair appears damp from his morning shower. The button-down shirt and tie he's wearing are immaculately pressed. He's clearly going into the office even though it's a Sunday. Dad's in a salaried position, which basically just means he puts in overtime for free.

"Thanks. Hopefully, the judges for the grant will think so too." I dip my finger in the dough and pop it into my mouth. It's fantastic, sweet and rich with a tang of salt. One of the great things about AIP baking is eggs aren't allowed, so cookie dough is free-game.

"Well, I'm sure they'd be crazy not to." Dad smiles, but his eyes have that pinched look they get whenever we talk about anything to do with money. "Listen, I have some bad news, sweetheart."

At my dad's serious tone, I set down my cookie dough and focus.

"We found out they're making some changes to our health plans at work next year. They're changing providers. The deductibles are going up, and—" Dad's voice trails off, and he swallows, looking at the ground. "The new plan won't cover your Cromolyn prescription."

The air leaves my lungs in a whoosh. I feel like I just got punched in the gut. Cromolyn is the most effective medication for controlling my condition, and it costs fourteen hundred dollars a month before insurance. Our current plan only pays about half of it, but the idea of having to come up with all that money on my own makes me nauseous.

"I'm so sorry," Dad says. "But don't worry. We'll figure something out." Guilt and worry are etched in the lines around his mouth. I hate that he feels bad about not being able to do more for me financially. Dad has nothing to feel guilty about. He works hard, and he's got a good job. It isn't his fault that the outrageous cost of living in New York is rivaled only by the expense of having a chronic illness in this country. Besides, I'm twenty-one years old. I knew I'd have to figure out how to foot the bill for my healthcare eventually. I just didn't expect to have to do it so soon.

"It's okay." I force a bright smile even though I feel hollow, like someone used my ice cream scoop to remove my insides. "We will figure it out. If I get this grant, I'll be able to launch my business. I'll be living a life of luxury before you know it."

"That's the spirit." Dad's smile looks as fake as my own.

My timer blares. I grab my mitt off the counter and peek inside the stainless-steel oven. It's by far the nicest appliance I own. Walking into my kitchen is like entering the Land of Misfit Gadgets. The microwave is flimsy, white plastic with a crack across the front. The old-fashioned farmhouse sink is made out of green ceramic. And the refrigerator looks like something that arrived in the back of Marty McFly's DeLorean. It has to be straight out of 1955. The pool house was unfurnished when I moved in. I bought everything second-hand with quite a bit of help from Betty and Dad.

The intoxicating smell of gooey, melted chocolate and toasted sugar floods the room. I set the cookies on top of the stove to cool. They're utter perfection, fluffy with a crisp, golden crust. Unfortunately, this is the batch of regular cookies I'm pitting against my AIP version to convince the good people of Rosedale that sugar-free is the way to be. I frown. I may have self-sabotaged with these. They look too good. I sigh and pop the AIP batch into the oven.

"So, how are things with Carrie?" I try to ignore the lead weight of panic lodged in my gut and switch the topic to something only slightly less complicated.

To say Carrie and I didn't hit it off is an understatement. Convinced I was exaggerating my gluten intolerance, she snuck bread crumbs into the meatballs she made when Dad took me to meet her. Within five minutes, I was covered in hives and had a migraine that lasted three days.

Despite that, I'm glad my dad has someone. I worry about him alone up there in the city without me. Carrie's the first official girlfriend he's had since my mom died. She's an executive assistant at a major law firm. She works long hours, so Dad's workaholic tendencies aren't a problem for her like they were for other women he's dated.

"She's good." A grin stretches across Dad's face. Even if the two of us are unlikely to ever be besties, it makes my heart happy that Carrie can make him smile like that. "She's doing a yoga class in Central Park this morning."

"That sounds very health-conscious. Maybe you should join her sometime."

"I'll have to think about that." Dad gives a weak chuckle and nods. "Well, you're pretty busy over there, kiddo. And I should probably head. Call me tomorrow morning? I want to hear all about the bake sale."

"You got it." I turn back to the screen. "Please try not to worry too much about the insurance thing. We've got months to figure it out."

Dad gives me a half-hearted smile. "I'll do my best. Love you, hun."

"Love you." I blow a kiss at the phone, and Dad winks at me.

I keep my smile fixed in place until his face disappears, then I bury my face in my hands.

This can't be happening. I probably haven't got an ice dancer's chance in hell at getting picked for the grant. And when I get reject-ed, my dad will feel even guiltier about not being able to help me. There's no way I can afford my prescriptions and the licenses and insurance I need to start my business. I could talk to Paula about a loan, but I don't have any credit. There's no way I'd qualify.

I love working at Giselle's and plan to keep teaching classes even if I do become a nutrition counselor. But without help from our insurance provider, the cost of my medication will by far exceed what I make there. I'll have to get a second job.

I give myself ten seconds to feel the sheer terror over my impending financial situation. Then I take a deep breath and shake out my arms, trying to rally. "Okay, pity party over," I tell myself. This is a setback, but I have a plan. I just need to stick to the plan. My tuition is already paid for, so I'm going to finish my nutrition certification. And I will submit the best application I can for that grant to give myself a fighting chance.

I inhale a deep breath to calm my nerves. But instead of the scrumptious scent of freshly baked chocolate chip cookies, I get a noseful of smoke.

Oh, shoot. I forgot to set the timer!

I spin around. Tendrils of gray slither out of the oven and into the air. "No! No! No!"

Shoving on my mitt, I pull the charred cookies out of the oven and rush to the window. I open it wide, wafting the smoke outside before the alarm goes off. I glance at my watch. 11:38. I haven't got time to make another batch before I need to leave for the bake sale. Talk about an epic backfire. My AIP cookies—the ones for my grant application—resemble bricks of charcoal, while my plain, sugar-loaded cookies look fantastic.

My phone vibrates on the counter. I trudge over to it, feet dragging against the tile in defeat. It's a text from Janet.

Janet: Hi, Quinn! Remember, everything you can imagine can be real.

I let my head fall backward and moan. Unless it's possible to imagine my cookies un-burning themselves, I am so screwed.

Chapter 12

My table is by far the most Instagram-worthy setup in the park. The iridescent, rose-colored tablecloth shimmers in the sunlight that filters through the canopy of leaves overhead. I arranged gold paper plates in diagonal lines across the table. Each plate has one regular and one AIP cookie, which I wrapped in cellophane and secured with a sparkly ribbon. I propped up a pink, felt letter board that reads, 'Can you tell which cookie is sugar-free?' I even put out a couple vases of peonies that I clipped from Betty's garden.

I've taken plenty of pictures to include with my grant application, but I don't think they'll do much to sway the judges' opinions. I hoped to take videos of people sampling both cookies and declaring the sugar-free version the better of the two. But the odds of that happening are looking slimmer by the second.

Kallie Peters was my first customer. She took one bite of the scorched AIP cookie and immediately started coughing. Nearly lighting them on fire earlier must have dried them out. Thankfully,

Giselle had the presence of mind to rush over with a water bottle before Kallie legit choked.

Word must have spread—as it's been known to do here in Rosedale. Not one person has stopped by my table in the past hour unless you count Liv and Betty. They devoured a couple of my regular cookies and tried to hype me up, loudly exclaiming over how "utterly delectable" they were. But the rest of the town is carefully avoiding making eye contact with me. Their gazes flick straight from Shirley Nelson's cupcakes on my left to Ty's cannolis on my right.

Shirley's got an unfair advantage, being the owner of the bakery. Her table is brimming with cupcakes decorated to look like the sunflowers in the giant fields that surround Rosedale. The centers are made of chocolate sprinkles, and the frosted, yellow petals are so life-like they're more like a work of art than a dessert. Her line hasn't dwindled since the bake sale started.

To my never-ending irritation, the line at Ty's table is even longer. He didn't put any effort into this. He hasn't laid down so much as a tablecloth, and I know for a fact that his mother, Lucia, made those cannolis. I can smell the mouth-watering fried pastry dough and ricotta filling from here. Lucia's cannolis are unparalleled. I've risked a flare-up more than once for them. If Lucia was here selling them instead of Ty, I'd probably do it again.

I drum my fingers against my thighs and scowl over at him. He passes cannolis to Faris and Amala Reddy. Naturally, he doesn't even have napkins to give them. I roll my eyes. The Reddys don't seem to mind, though. They each take a bite, and their eyes light up like fireflies on a warm summer night. Ty slides a clipboard across the table and hands Amala a pen.

What's that about? I wonder, leaning sideways on my folding chair to hear what he's saying.

"The Bourne Identity was one of the highest-grossing movies of 2002, and I've heard the kissing scenes in Ever After are a little steamy. We have to think about the children." He gestures at the stroller Faris has been pushing through the park.

I gasp so hard I choke on my own saliva. Sputtering and coughing, my eyes water as I attempt to suck in air. I cannot believe him. He's using his mother's cannolis to convince the town to vote for his movie. He's diabolical.

Giselle hustles over with another water. She uncaps the bottle, handing it to me and patting my back as I try to get my breathing under control. "Did you eat one of the cookies?" she asks.

I glare at her with as much heat as I can muster while tears stream down my face. "No, I didn't eat one of the cookies."

"Oh, good." She places a hand to her chest as though relieved. She's wearing a gorgeous, bohemian-style turquoise dress. Her hair is down in beachy waves. She looks like she just stepped out of a Pinterest ad.

I sigh. "The cookies aren't that bad. They're just a little over-baked."

Giselle gives me the side-eye. And, okay, who am I trying to kid here? Giselle's a professionally trained chef.

"Fine," I admit. "They're burned."

"Well, stop eating them then."

"I wasn't. I just—" I fling an arm toward Ty. "He's over there trying to steal everyone's votes for the movie in the park."

"Oh, yes." Giselle brightens. "Did you know The Bourne Identity won Best Action Sequence of 2002 for the car chase scene? I had no idea."

"Not you, too," I groan.

"What? Do you not like car chases?" Giselle's forehead bunches in confusion. "Who doesn't like car chases?"

"I don't have anything against car chases. I—" My words trail off as I glance over at Ty's table where Amala is scribbling something on the clipboard, no doubt voting for his stupid movie."Giselle, I've got to go take care of something."

"Do you want me to watch your table for you?"

I cast a glance around the crowded park. Couples hold hands, wandering between the tables. Kids run around screaming, their faces covered in chocolate. I can see Betty and Liv darting back and forth across the lawn, buying up all the snacks they can get their hands on. But my table is deserted.

"I don't think that's necessary, but thanks, Giselle."

"Anytime," she calls after me as I cut a bee-line toward Ty. The sky is a bright, clear blue. Sunshine kisses the spaces of grass the giant maple trees don't shade. At least it's cooled down a bit. This place would be a puddle of melted frosting if it was as hot as yesterday.

"You made the right choice." Ty smiles hugely at Amala as she passes the clipboard back to him. She grabs another cannoli and shoves a dollar into the jar sitting in the center of his table. All the money raised today is being donated to the elementary school for new textbooks. Ty's jar is overflowing while I've brought in a grand total of three dollars.

"What do you think you're doing?" I put my hand on the hip of my mauve, high-waist shorts.

Ty looks over at me. His eyes skate over my legs before settling on my face, making warmth flood my cheeks. It's beyond irritating that he can still get me all flustered with a single look.

"I'm selling cannolis. I think the question is, what are you doing?" Ty jerks his chin toward my table of unsold cookies.

He turns back to his throng of customers and passes cannolis to Pete Winchester and Aaron Martinez. "Thanks, guys." He shoots them a grin as they add their money to his growing stash.

"Give our compliments to your mother." Pete takes a big bite. "These things are the bomb, man."

"Will do." Ty nods as Pete twines his fingers through Aaron's, and the two of them wander toward Shirley Nelson's table. They were voted prom king and king our senior year. It makes me happy to see them together still, even if the ending of my own high-school romance was apocalyptic.

"Where is your mom anyway?" I ask Ty.

He looks down at the basket of cannolis. "She's busy at the restaurant."

I frown. That's two events Lucia's missed in a row. I hope everything's going okay with their business. She's usually happy to close shop for the day to spend time with her family.

"Hey, Al. Have you voted for this year's movie in the park?" Ty points at the clipboard as Al from Al's Construction steps to the front of the line and takes a cannoli out of the basket. "I heard that The Bourne Identity is one of the best thrillers of all time."

"You are such a cheater." I swipe the clipboard off the table.

"How am I cheating? I told you I wanted to poll everyone during the events this week." Ty reaches for the clipboard, but I hold it behind my back, out of his reach.

"But you failed to mention that you would actively campaign against me."

Al glances between Ty and me, looking uncomfortable. "Uh, thanks for the cannoli."

"No problem. Sorry about her." Ty gives my shoulder a patronizing pat. I jerk away. "You can come place your vote after the bossy train has exited the station."

There's an intake of breath from the crowd watching in line. I'm sure they're listening to every word, but I don't care. I'm not going to let Ty hijack the movie night. I cross my arms over the clipboard and glare at him.

"What?" he asks, looking far too pleased with himself. "I can't help it if people are more interested in watching my film than yours."

I look down at the paper he's been using to tally votes. There are at least twenty for The Bourne Identity and not a single one for Ever After.

Someone giggles, and I glance over to see Betty and Liv standing front and center in Ty's line. They're each munching on caramel corn and grinning like this whole situation is oh-so entertaining. I shake my head at them before turning back to Ty. "You're poisoning everyone against my movie."

Ty shrugs. "I'm just stating facts. But if you don't like the voting system, we can call it right now. The Bourne Identity is clearly going to win anyway."

I narrow my eyes at him. "I don't think so." I tug the piece of paper from beneath the clip, crumpling it.

"Oh, come on! I've been working on those votes all afternoon."

I shove the clipboard against Ty's chest. "We're doing a re-vote tomorrow at the rain gutter regatta. A fair one."

Ty shakes his head. "Fine. It's not like the results are going to be any different."

"We'll see about that." I nod toward the ever-growing mob watching us."You should get back to work. You've got customers."

I turn to go back to my own table and hear him mutter, "Unlike some people."

Oooh. I deserve an award for not strangling this boy. "Tomorrow, Rossi," I call over my shoulder like it's a threat.

"Can't wait, Kelley."

Chapter 13

The printer whirs and clicks in the corner of Betty's home office as it spits out the homemade flyers we've been working on all evening.

I had a total meltdown when I got back from the bake sale. I sold just one other pair of cookies this afternoon. One. And that was only because Kelvin felt bad for me. He gave my regular cookie a rave review, but I saw him toss the AIP one in the trashcan on the other side of the park. I was in tears by the time I got home.

Even when you know something you made sucks, it still stings when other people agree with you. My big plan for demonstrating to the Happy Spoons judges that I'm helping others with my nutrition certification completely backfired. I have no idea what I can do to convince them to pick me now. And with the changes to our insurance plan, I really need that money. To top off the crap sundae that was my day, I only raised four dollars for the elementary school. Ty sold so many cannolis he probably funded a new library single-handedly.

Betty took one look at my tear-stained face when I got home and launched into problem-solving mode. Within an hour, we had delivery pizza for her and Liv, sweet potato curry for me, and a battle plan. I have to admit, it's solid.

Liv suggested that instead of the chocolate and avocado protein truffles I was planning to make for my class on Tuesday, I could allow people to bring their own recipes with them. That way, I can teach them how to modify the ingredients to make the dishes more inclusive.

Betty jumped on the idea like a bridesmaid going after a bouquet at a wedding. Now, not only do we have a strategy, we've got an entire marketing scheme. Betty made the flyers, which we're going to pass out during the rain gutter regatta tomorrow. Hopefully, come Tuesday morning, I'll have a classroom full of happy students who'll provide me with testimonials I can use for my grant application. For the first time, I think I might actually be in the running for this thing.

"Have I told you that you're my favorite person today?" I ask Liv. She's sitting next to me on the plush, gray carpet of Betty's office, cutting out the flyers. Betty printed four per page, so people can easily put them in their bags or pocket during the regatta.

"Only ten times in the past hour," Liv says. "But don't let that stop you." Her scissors snick, snick, snick against the paper.

"She's your favorite? What am I? Chopped liver?" Betty takes a bite of her now-cold pizza, washing it down with a gulp of a margarita and a piece of a sunflower cupcake. She dubbed today Snacks on Snacks Sunday because of the bake sale. Her and Liv's eating habits are always equal parts impressive and terrifying, and they're truly outdoing themselves tonight. If I didn't already know their stomachs were made of lead, I'd be concerned.

"You are prime rib. The finest of cuts," I say. "Also, you're the greatest aunt a girl could ask for. These flyers are perfect. Thank you."

"Ah, stahp. You're going to go and make me blush," Betty drawls in her best Southern accent. She's sitting in her ergonomic chair, with her feet resting on the desk. Her face glows in the light coming from her computer. She's been watching videos of raccoons devouring Cocoa Puffs since she finished designing the flyers. It's gotten dark outside, and the dim lighting washes out the pale blue paint on the walls.

"Can't stop. Won't stop." I hop up to flick on the lamp. "I seriously owe you two for this. I'd still be in a puddle of tears on the living room floor if it wasn't for you. Now I feel like I might have a shot at getting this grant for real."

I'm fizzy with excitement and anticipation, like someone's infused my bloodstream with sparklers.

The only person more thrilled about this idea than I am is Giselle. I texted her, so she could have the kitchen at the school stocked with all the supplies we'll need for recipe modifications. She called almost the instant the word 'delivered' popped up, confirming she'd received my text. She thinks the class will be a hit and wants to make it a weekly thing.

Giselle pays me by the hour, but I also get a percentage of the fee she charges each student per class. If it really does go well, I could scrape up enough to cover the increased costs of my prescriptions without getting a second job.

"Well, we're happy to help." Betty shoots me a warm smile, then she claps her hands together. "Enough of the mushy stuff. Let's talk tactics. What's the plan for tomorrow?"

"I'm going to hand out as many flyers as possible while Ty and I get everyone's votes for the movie night. If you two can make sure everybody gets one and encourage them to come to the class, that would be awesome."

"You're in luck. Annoying people into doing things happens to be one of our specialties." Liv bites into a brownie. She's got a horde of baked goods spread out on the floor in front of her. I'm eternally grateful there isn't a single cannoli insight. It sets my teeth on edge just thinking about Ty being all pleased with himself for his cannoli sales and duplicitous movie votes.

"Well, no matter how annoying you two think you are, you've got nothing on Ty. Can you believe that guy? Trying to trick everyone into voting for his movie." Grabbing another sheet of paper, I carefully cut the flyers, making sure the lines are even. I drop them on the pile and notice Betty and Liv exchange a look.

I glance back and forth between them. They catch me watching them and go back to stuffing their faces with snacks. The atmosphere in the room is charged, like they have a secret I'm not in on.

"Okay, what's with the look?"

"What look?" Liv asks around a mouthful of brownie.

I set my scissors on the floor, staring her down. "You know what look."

"Well, it's just—" Liv begins, and Betty huffs out a here-we-go kind of sigh. "We were thinking—"

"Wondering," Betty corrects.

"Right. We were wondering," Liv continues, "if maybe, possibly, you and Ty might still have feelings for each other." She says the last part so quickly it takes a second for the meaning of her words to hit me.

When it does, I gasp. I'm so stunned that I start choking on my own saliva for the second time in less than eight hours. I didn't know it was possible to kill someone with their own spit, but after today, Betty, Liv, and Ty should all be brought up on attempted murder charges.

I snatch my Stanley cup off the carpet and take a gulp.

"It was just a thought." Liv winces as she pats my back.

"Well, un-cough-think it." My chest heaves as my breathing slowly returns to normal. "That ship sunk years ago. There's probably barnacles growing over the wreckage by now."

"Alright," Betty says placatingly. "We believe you. It seemed like there might still be some sparks happening there." I start to argue, but she holds up a hand. "But clearly, we were wrong."

"Very, very wrong." I cross my legs underneath me and narrow my eyes at them. "There are no sparks between Ty and me. None. Zero sparking happening. We are never getting back together."

Liv opens her mouth like she's got something else to say, but Betty gives her a look, and she snaps it shut.

The three of us lapse into silence. The printer finishes the last of the flyers, and Betty hands them to us. I take a sheet and am about to put scissors to it when Liv's cell phone buzzes loudly on the floor next to us. She snatches it off the ground. Her eyes dance over the screen, going wide. She squeals and leaps to her feet.

"Oh, my God. You got it?" Betty stands so quickly her chair slides backward and ricochets off the wall.

"I got it!" Liv starts jumping up and down. Betty and I scream and pounce on her, squashing her in a massive group hug. "You're looking at the next Kappa Zeta president!" Liv cries.

Betty presses a kiss to Liv's head. "I am so proud of you!" Then she turns to me and plants one on me too. "And I'm so proud of you. Look out, world. The Kelley girls are coming for you!"

Chapter 14

"**D**id you know there are twenty-nine swear words in The Bourne Identity? Twenty-nine. And that includes an f-word." I open my eyes wide, fluttering my lashes. I need to convince the parents of Rosedale to vote for my movie if I'm going to win, so I'm working the innocent, doe-eyed girl angle hard. I even dressed the part. Betty let me borrow her yellow, babydoll-style dress, and I kept my makeup simple. Just a swipe of mascara and a tiny bit of pink gloss.

"Didn't we vote yesterday?" Faris Reddy scratches his cheek, studying the clipboard I'm holding toward him.

Ty and I have been canvassing Winchester Market's parking lot all morning, polling everyone. The store is closed to host today's event. According to Paula's binder, the asphalt behind Winchester's is the levelest ground in Rosedale and, therefore, the best location for a rain gutter regatta.

Rows of gutters filled with water are lined up across the lot. People surround them, cheering on the toy boats. Kids use straws to blow the sails, racing to the end of the tracks. Liv and Betty wander between the groups, discreetly slipping flyers for my class into people's bags and strollers.

"You did vote already, Mr. Reddy." Ty takes the clipboard from my hand. "And you made the right decision. I heard Angelica Houston was nominated for an award called Choice-Sleazebag for Ever After. Does that sound like a family-friendly film to you?"

"The previous voting system was flawed." I snatch the clipboard back. "And that was a Teen Choice Award for her outstanding performance as the film's villain. It was an honor."

"I mean, if you think being called sleazy is an honor..." Ty lifts a brow, giving the Reddys a look that clearly says, can you believe this Jezebel?

I must have the self-discipline of Maria Sharapova because there are several insults on the tip of my tongue, and I manage not to hurl a single one of them at Ty. A breeze whips past, blowing strands of hair across my face and making them stick to my lipgloss. I swipe at them as a cheer echoes through the parking lot.

"That's not fair!" Gary hollers. "The wind totally pushed Tommy's boat across the finish line."

"We can't control the wind, Gary," Betty says. "Now, be a good sport and stop pouting over losing to an eight-year-old."

I stifle a smirk and turn my attention back to the Reddys.

"Maybe we should skip movie night this year." Amala's forehead furrows as she looks at the thick clouds blotting out the sunshine. They're getting darker and more sinister by the minute.

"That might be a good idea." Faris grabs the handles of their stroller and goes to steer it around Ty.

Crap. As much as I want my film to beat Ty's, I don't want our trash-talking to discourage people from attending the event. Paula would kill us if she found out we sabotaged it.

"No, no." I jump into Faris's path. "You can't miss movie night. It's the highlight of the festival, and Giselle's pulling out all the stops on the catering. Rumor has it she's making her famous popcorn balls."

"We'll think about it." Faris's tone is flat, like his mind is already made up.

"Please do," Ty says as the Reddys start to walk away again.

Apparently, I don't know when to quit, though. "Wait!" I yell and fish a flyer from the tote bag looped over my shoulder. I thrust it toward Amala. "If you're free tomorrow, I'm teaching a class on modifying your favorite recipes to accommodate any dietary restrictions. It'll be fuuuun." I must be possessed because I throw in an eyebrow waggle as I say the word 'fun.'

Faris wraps a protective arm around Amala's shoulders like he thinks I pose some kind of danger to her. "We'd really rather not." He frowns at me, and they brush past without another glance in my direction.

Between the eyebrow waggle and the slightly hysterical pitch of my voice, I don't blame them. But it's hard to be calm and collected when I'm desperate for people to attend my class. Liv's decided to broadcast the whole thing on Instagram Live for my followers. She thinks it'll be a great way to demonstrate how I'm using what I've learned in my nutrition courses to help people both here in my community and online. But if I don't have a decent turnout, I will look like such a poser.

Ty scoffs behind me. "Nice work."

"Well, it's not like you were helping with your sleazebag comment.." I turn, scowling at him. "How much time did you spend researching horrible facts about my movie, anyway?"

Ty puts his hands on his hips and leans toward me. "I'll put as much time into this as it takes. At least one of us is committed to making the movie night a success."

"You should be committed," I grumble, watching a man in a clown costume fold a balloon into the shape of a kitten. He hands it to a little girl just as another gust of wind rips through the lot. It sends the balloon flying into the air and catches at the skirt of my dress. I grab the hem with my free hand, tugging it down as the girl starts sobbing. I dart a look up at the darkening sky. We will need to pull the plug on this regatta if the weather gets any worse.

"You two are actually scaring people. You do realize that, right?" I turn to see Ty's sister, Francie, striding toward us. She must be working the lunch shift because she's wearing her black 'Rossi's' t-shirt. Gianna and Lisa are right behind her.

"Well, hello there, pretty ladies." I flash them my most charming smile and hold out the clipboard. "Did you know Drew Barrymore once said that Ever After is her favorite movie she's ever starred in?"

"You can save the speech." Lisa takes the clipboard from my hands and uncaps the pen I've attached to it. "We're voting for Ever After."

"Hey!" Ty lunges for the clipboard, but Lisa passes it behind her to Gianna.

"I'm sorry, but we are not watching The Bourne Identity again. If I have to sit through that car chase one more time, I swear to Mother Mary..." Gianna jots down her vote. I've always adored Gianna. She's like the big sister I never had. Even now, she comments on every single one of my Instagram posts.

"I can't believe this," Ty says. "Haven't you three ever heard that blood is thicker than water?"

"Haven't you ever heard that sisters come before misters?" Francie scribbles on the board and gives it back to me.

Ty jerks a thumb toward me. "She isn't your sister."

"And whose fault is that?" Gianna shoots Ty a pointed look. She's seven years older than us and a total romantic. She was planning our future wedding before we even officially started dating.

"Hers," Ty says at the same time I say, "His."

Lisa glances between the two of us and shakes her head. "We need to get back to the restaurant. We just wanted to stop by and cast our votes." She unties the cardigan from around her waist and slips her arms into it.

"Try not to murder each other while you're unsupervised," Francie says. "And maybe don't talk everyone out of coming to the movie night. Otherwise, I don't want to be anywhere near you two when Paula gets back." Her long hair tangles in the wind, and she plucks the elastic band off her wrist, tying it into a messy bun.

"I'll do my best, but no promises about the murder thing." I tuck the clipboard under my arm and fish out a stack of flyers from my tote. "Would you mind putting these on the counter at Rossi's for me? They're flyers for my class tomorrow."

"Sure thing, hun." Lisa takes the flyers and turns to her sisters. "Let's go. Dad's probably swamped, and it's freezing out here."

They hurry back toward Main Street, and Gianna blows us a kiss over her shoulder.

"Thank you!" I shout after them.

"Unbelievable," Ty mutters, watching them go. "Betrayed by my own sisters."

"Can't win 'em all." I pat him on the arm. I'm surprised all over again by how muscular he's gotten. We never unfollowed each other on social media, so I've seen plenty of pictures of him over the years we've been apart, but they did not do those muscles of his justice. I pull my hand back, wrapping my arms around myself and shivering. Goosebumps spring up across my bare legs.

A fat raindrop plops against my forehead, and I wipe it away with my fingertips.

"Do you think we should call it?" I ask Ty. All around us, people are grabbing their sailboats and children, heading for higher ground.

Ty follows my gaze, nodding. "It's not exactly regatta weather. I think we got most everyone's votes anyw—" Ty's words trail off as his eyes lock on something over my shoulder.

"What?" I turn to see what he's looking at.

But it isn't a what. It's a who. Old Man Jenkins. He's scuttling across the parking lot at a quick clip for a ninety-seven-year-old man. Old Man Jenkins rarely leaves his house anymore. I haven't seen him around town in months. I didn't expect him to be at any of the events this week, but since Tommy Jenkins is his grandson, it makes sense that he'd make the effort to come and watch him race. I'm surprised I didn't spot that all-white pompadour of his earlier. He must have snuck in while Ty and I were talking to the Reddys.

And while I'd love to be a big enough person to drop the whole vote thing and let Ty have his stupid movie, I'm just not. I don't know if it's because I'm still mad about what happened in high school, and this is the only way I can think of to get back at him, or if it's because it doesn't feel like the town's just voting on a film anymore. It feels like they're picking sides between Ty and me.

Whatever the reason, all I know is that I have to win. And as close as this race is, every vote counts. This is my only chance to convince Old Man Jenkins to pick my movie.

Slowly, I turn toward Ty. Our eyes lock, and I can tell from the mischievous twist to his lips that he's thinking the same thing. Before Ty can so much as blink, I take off running, chasing Old Man Jenkins across the parking lot.

Chapter 15

I sprint through the parking lot. My shimmery, gold sandals slap against the asphalt. Raindrops speckle my face as I dodge people fleeing the storm. My arms pump, and my skin chafes against my wet tote bag. The wind whooshes past my ears, but I can still hear Ty's sneakers squeaking on the blacktop behind me.

Not today, Satan, I think. No way am I letting Ty sweet-talk Old Man Jenkins into voting for his dumb movie.

I dig deep, sprinting with all I've got. I haven't run like this since I was a child, and for some reason, I remember it being much more enjoyable. My lungs burn, straining for oxygen, and my head throbs with the pounding of my heart.

I squint through the rain coming down in earnest now, making my dress stick to my legs. Old Man Jenkins is halfway across the street. Dang. That is one fast old dude.

Ty's stride is a lot longer than mine, and despite all my effort, he's easily keeping up with me. I run harder, muscles screaming from exertion. But from the corner of my eye, I see him start to pull ahead.

Linda Blair has nothing on me. If I thought I was possessed earlier, I'm certain of it now. I swear, I have absolutely no control over my elbow as it flings itself outward, colliding into Ty's arm hard enough to make him stumble.

"Quinn!" He shouts after me as I dash down the sidewalk, kicking up a spray of water. Ty hasn't given up, though. I hadn't heard any rumors about him joining the track team out at UCLA, but I'm starting to wonder because he quickly catches up to me.

Too bad for him, this demon has a firm hold on me. My elbow nails him again, nearly knocking him into the slick cobblestone street.

"Quinn, stop! I can't push you back. You're a girl."

"Well, it sucks to suck!" I yell as I sprint into the road.

Ty must have the tenacity of a honey badger because he closes the gap between us again. I attempt to throw another elbow, but he dodges it this time. I overbalance, tripping as my shoes skid on the wet stones. My tote bag flies off my arm, sending flyers scattering over the sodden street. The clipboard slides out of my grip as I crash into Ty like a defensive tackle taking down a quarterback.

Ty takes the brunt of the fall, landing on his back and elbows. He lets out an oof as the air is knocked from his lungs. I land on top of him, arms and legs wrapped around his body like a spider monkey. I scramble to push myself off, but my hand slips on the stones, and I fall against him. Our heads smash into each other with a loud thunk. The heel of my palm burns where it skidded against the street.

"Ouch." Ty rubs his knuckles against his forehead, struggling to sit up. "For the record, this is all your fault. But are you okay?" His eyes rove over my face and the skin of my arms as though checking for damage.

I'm suddenly very aware of my wet dress, clinging to every curve of my body. Judging by the way Ty's gaze keeps drifting downward, so is he. I feel exposed, like he can see every inch of me. Like he can see right through me. Our chests rise and fall together as we try to catch our breath.

"I'm, uh...I'm fine. Great." I grapple to a standing position, tugging on my waterlogged skirt with one hand and reaching down to help Ty with the other.

He examines my outstretched palm like he thinks it's some kind of trap. Finally, his fingers close around mine, and I pull him to his feet.

"You're a hazard to the entire town." Ty shakes his head at me, but there's a spark of amusement in his eyes. Drops of water cling to his eyelashes. I'm finding it overwhelmingly difficult to look away from them. I try to think of some witty comeback, but I've got nothing.

We stand in the rain, staring at each other. The adrenaline from our footrace is thrumming through my system, and the rush of emotions that always fills me when I'm this close to Ty is a live wire. The air around us is charged with the electricity of it. It's heartache, and possibility, and attraction like I've never experienced with anyone else. But the hurt and confusion are there too. It's all so much to feel at once; it doesn't seem possible to contain it all inside me.

Ty's hand twitches at his side like he wants to reach for me, but a car horn blares, echoing through the town square. We spring apart like middle schoolers caught making out under the bleachers.

"Unless you two are reenacting that scene from The Notebook, can we move this show indoors? People are trying to drive here," Betty yells from the window of her Prius, idling in the road.

"Coming," I call, glancing back at Ty. He rakes his fingers through his hair, pushing it out of his eyes. I try really hard not to think about how much I want to run my own fingers through that hair. It's a good thing it's raining because, apparently, I need a cold shower.

I clear my throat. "Do you want a ride?" I nod toward Betty's Prius.

"I'm good to walk. I'm just going to the restaurant." Ty shoves his hands in his pocket, eyes dropping to the ground like he feels as uncomfortable as I do. "Thanks, though."

I'm oddly disappointed, like he's rejecting me and not a car ride. "You bet." I force a smile." I'll see you tomorrow, then."

For some reason, it feels weird to just turn and walk away. Hugging him goodbye is so deeply ingrained in my DNA that it's become routine, but there's no way I'm about to do that. All the rain must have water-logged my brain because the best thing I can come up with is holding my hand out for a high five.

Ty glances from my face to my palm. A smirk curls the edge of his lips. "Yeah. See you then." He slaps my hand, trying and failing to hide a chuckle.

Ugh. If being the most awkward human on the planet was an Olympic sport, I'd be a gold medalist. I turn on my heel and pluck my clipboard out of a puddle. Inky water runs in rivulets over the pages, making it impossible to read. Freaking fantastic.

Without looking back at Ty, I dash across the road and tug open the door of Betty's car, jumping into the backseat.

"Someone had better call Guinness because I'm pretty sure you two just set the world record for the lamest high five in history." Betty's eyes meet mine in the rearview mirror. "What was up with that?"

I groan, burying my face in my hands. "I have no idea."

Liv turns around in the passenger seat and pats my shoulder. "Yeah, it's a total mystery. You know, since the two of you clearly don't have feelings for each other anymore."

I glare at her through my fingers. I'd need a freaking roadmap to navigate my feelings for Ty, but I'm too cold and wet to pretend they don't exist right now.

Chapter 16

I 've never related to that stupid rabbit from Alice in Wonderland more. The words I'm late! I'm late! I'm late! loop through my mind as I sprint through the park. My hair flies behind me. It's probably tangling itself into a giant knot, which I believe is what they call karma.

I was such a nervous wreck over teaching a classroom full of my friends and neighbors that I fell down my own rabbit hole of self-doubt. I curled and re-curled my hair at least seven times until it hung in perfect, golden waves over my shoulders. And that was after I spent an hour on my makeup.

The idea of so many people watching me both here and over the internet is completely wigging me out. I wish I didn't care so much about what all those people will think of me, but I do. I'm doing everything in my power to control their perception of me and simultaneously turning myself into an anxiety pretzel.

I took my usual dose of Cromolyn with a Benadryl, which I usually reserve for emergency situations—aka anaphylaxis. But I didn't want to risk a repeat of the whole shaky legs incident. Especially since there's a slim chance that one of the judges for the Happy Spoons Grant could be watching online.

I dodge the drips of rainwater falling from the leaves of the maple trees. It's a sunny, cloudless morning, but everything is still damp from yesterday's storm. My sandals are soaked through, so I'm careful as I run across the street. The last thing I need is to slip on one of the cobblestones again. Those things are becoming less charming by the day, let me tell you.

I reach the sidewalk and freeze. Giselle has the barn doors of the school closed, and there's a line of people waiting out front that snakes around the corner of the building. My pulse thuds against my throat, and I'm suddenly finding it hard to swallow.

What have I gotten myself into? I expected fifteen people tops. But there are at least thirty people out here. They'll need to put three people at each station, and someone else is definitely going to be teaching because I cannot do this.

I'm considering running straight back home and hiding under my comforter when I spot Liv. She's standing in front of the school, scanning the sidewalk—probably searching for me. Her eyes lock on mine, and she shoots a hand in the air, waving.

"Quinn! Get your cute butt over here. Everyone's waiting for you."

"That's what I was afraid of," I mutter. But I force myself to smile, trying to look enthusiastic about the turnout. Liv and Betty put so much effort into making this class a success I don't want to be ungrateful. But I also don't want to vomit on Instagram Live, which is becoming a more real possibility by the second. My stomach twists, and I'm seriously regretting that zucchini and dark chocolate chip muffin I ate for breakfast.

"What happened? When we left, you said you were right behind us. That was forty-five minutes ago." Liv links her arm through mine, tugging me toward the classroom. We speed-walk past the line of people chatting and laughing. Some of them give me big smiles, looking way too excited about getting this show on the road. No pressure.

"I just, um. Well—" I swirl my hand in front of my face, gesturing at my makeup. The old, wooden steps groan beneath us, and Liv slides open the heavy door. We hurry inside, not bothering to shut it after us since class is about to start.

"Right." Liv nods. "You look—" Her eyes drift from my face to the disaster that is my hair. "Well, we'll work on it. You've still got a couple of minutes before your class. I have the tripod set up, and Giselle has everything ready. I just need your phone."

"My phone?"

"For Instagram Live." Liv raises her eyebrows like I'm being deliberately slow. She's not far from the mark. My brain feels like it's slogging through quicksand. All I can think about are all the eyes that will be watching me inside the classroom. Forget the thousands of people that will potentially be tuning in online.

I open my mouth, but words don't come out. The threat of that muffin making a reappearance seems imminent.

"Quinn?" Liv grabs my hands, which are slowly going numb. Her gaze darts back and forth between my eyes. "Quinn, you need to breathe."

I nod my head, but the motion only makes me more nauseous.

"Quinn, you're late. You should've been here an hour ago." Giselle strides toward us, examining the rows of cooking stations. The stainless steel ovens gleam in the fluorescent overhead lighting, and the counters are buffed to a high sheen. Each station is stocked with a wooden crate. I'm assuming they're full of sweet potatoes, coconut oil, and cassava flour, which are the staples of my diet. The smell of cinnamon and honey lingers in the air.

When I don't say anything, Giselle looks over at me. "You look sick." She turns to Liv. "Is she sick?"

"She has a thing about public speaking." Liv tugs her fingers through my hair, smoothing it out. "Mom, can we get some water over here?" she calls over her shoulder.

Betty's lugging a box of dates between the stations, adding a handful to each crate. She takes one look at me and sets the box down. "Oh, boy." She rushes toward the refrigerators at the back of the classroom, where a drop cloth covers the wall, blocking off the addition that's under construction.

Giselle must have kicked Al's team out for the class this morning. The persistent thumping of hammers and buzzing of saws is gone, leaving only the hum of the freezers and fluorescent lighting overhead.

"You're afraid of public speaking, and I'm just finding out about it now?" Giselle drags over a stool and places a hand on my shoulder, forcing me to sit.

"There aren't usually very many people in my classes." I shrug weakly.

Giselle mutters something in Portuguese, and I suck in a lungful of air, trying to slow the thrumming of my heart.

Before Betty can return with my water, Jenny Jenkins hurries over. Jenny owns Miss Jenny's Boutique on Main Street, and she's Old Man Jenkins's daughter. She must have been watching us from outside.

"Oh, dear. Quinn, are you alright? You poor thing. Here take this." She uncaps a bottle of water and thrusts it toward me. To my intense humiliation, she reaches out, setting her palm against my forehead like I'm a child she's checking for a fever.

I have a large personal bubble, and I don't like being touched by anyone except the select few humans in my inner circle. I've known Jenny for years, but we aren't close. I jerk my head away, but she doesn't take the hint. Her fingers clamp around my wrist, pressing into my pulse point. She stares down at her watch, counting.

Betty arrives with the water glancing from Jenny to the horrified expression on my face. She hangs her head in secondhand embarrassment and sighs.

"Jenny," she says, giving Jenny a firm tap on the shoulder. "We appreciate you watching out for Quinn, but she's fine." Liv and I are the only ones who can tell how forced the patience in Betty's voice is.

"Oh, of course." Jenny laughs. "You would know, Dr. Kelley." She turns her bright smile on me. "Gosh, it must be so nice to have an aunt who's a doctor when you're a sick girl."

It takes all my self-control not to roll my eyes. When people who aren't familiar with chronic health issues find out you have one, they react in one of two ways. They either think you're exaggerating your symptoms and need to "toughen up." Or they treat you like you're a complete invalid. Jenny's always been in the second camp, asking me if I'm "hanging in there okay."

Her heart's in the right place, and I'm grateful she cares. I am. But I've worked hard to get my condition under control. I manage it well now. For the most part, I live a normal life. I've even been able to add a lot of food items back into my diet and rarely have reactions these days. Having an ailment is nothing to be ashamed of, but I feel like I should be the one who gets to decide what defines me. And while my illness will always be part of who I am, I don't view myself as a sick girl. I hate that other people do.

Betty's well aware of my feelings on the matter and, thankfully, intercedes before my tolerance with Jenny runs out. "Well, someone needs to get ready if we're going to get this class started anytime soon." She wraps an arm around my shoulders, helping me to my feet.

Jenny's hovering has the unexpected side effect of distracting me from my stage fright. My stomach is distinctly less wobbly as I follow Betty to the front of the classroom. My nervousness has been replaced by a spark of determination. If I want people to stop thinking of me as an invalid, then I need to show them just how strong I am. I'm going to stand up here and teach these people how to eat themselves to a better life, and I will not vomit in the process.

I examine the ingredients spread across my workstation. Each one is set out next to items I use for substitutions: coconut oil for butter, agave for processed sugar, and cassava for all-purpose flour. I nod. This is going to be great. I can totally handle this.

"You look less green." Giselle sets a water on my station, examining my face. "For a second there, I was worried Gary might have shared his sunblock with you. Are you ready?" She tilts her head toward the line of people waiting at the open front door. We're a few minutes past the scheduled start time, and they're getting impatient. People stand on tiptoes, craning to get a peek inside and see what's causing the holdup.

A jolt of nerves crackles through my system, but I breathe through it and shake out my arms. "I'm ready."

"Here we go, then." Giselle walks over to the door and starts checking people in.

Liv hustles over to me. "Phone?" She holds her hand out. I slide it out of my pocket, passing it to her with only the slightest tremble in my fingers. Liv clips it into the tripod she's set up in the center aisle that divides the workstations. It's close enough that Instagram Live viewers will be able to see me clearly, as well as the first couple of rows of students.

Liv punches in the passcode on my phone and taps the screen, starting the broadcast. I take a gulp from my water bottle, swallowing my lingering anxiety as everyone files into the room. Betty and Liv take one of the stations in the front row, knowing I'll need friendly faces close by if I start getting nervous again. I shoot them a grateful smile.

Don't think about the camera. Don't think about the grant, I tell myself. Focus on sharing what you've learned. You know what you're talking about. You can do this.

My confidence in my own knowledge is beginning to win the tug-of-war with my fear of public speaking when the last people I ever expected to see inside a cooking classroom come strolling in. They claim the station right behind Liv and Betty. It's Chance, Kelvin, and, of course, Ty.

Chapter 17

I 'm too stunned to speak. Those three belong in this classroom as much as mustard belongs on pumpkin pie. My surprise is quickly replaced by fury, though. Because there's no way Ty, Chance, and Kelvin would ever willingly attend a baking class unless they had ulterior motives.

With the deadline for my grant application fast approaching, my future could be riding on the success of this class. The last thing I need is for a fake snake to come springing out of a pot or for someone's cassava flour to get mysteriously swapped with powdered sugar. I need to nip whatever sideshow they've planned in the bud before they can humiliate me in front of the entire internet.

My eyes dart to where my phone's propped on the tripod, broadcasting live over Instagram. I force a smile and speed-walk over to their workstation. Chance's nose is wrinkled as he examines a bottle of agave.

"Hey." Ty's smile is so full of warmth and sincerity I almost fall for it. But I know these boys and their pranks better than anyone. And they aren't here out of the goodness of their hearts.

"What are you doing?" I hiss, trying to keep my voice low as the room fills, and everyone takes out their recipes. Somehow, I need to get the three stooges out of here without creating a spectacle.

Ty's eyebrows furrow. "I'm here for your class." He pulls a piece of paper out of his pocket and unfolds it, smoothing it on the counter. My heart stutters when I see what it is—a recipe for his mother's coffee cake.

When we were together, the two of us spent weeks figuring out how to make a version of that cake that I wouldn't react to. Maintaining the flavor while substituting ingredients was a challenge. And it used to be my favorite thing in the world. Not only because it was delicious but because Ty helped me figure out how to make it safe for me to eat. It was ours, something we created together. I can't believe he'd bring it here.

He was there yesterday when I was passing out flyers, trying to convince everyone to come to my class. He knows how crucial this is for me. Now he's using that recipe to what? Try and trick me into relaxing my defenses?

I've been down this road with him plenty of times before, and I know where it leads. Someone will have a rubber rat on their station instead of a spatula or frosting that tastes strangely like toothpaste. And despite what they obviously think, I'm not dumb. I'm not about to fall for it. Not again.

"Out." I hold out my arm, pointing at the front door. "Get. Out."

"What?" Ty stares at me like I've lost my mind.

Chance and Kelvin snicker, and I shoot a seething glare over at them. Kelvin's holding a pair of dates in his hand. "They're like wrinkly, old man balls," he says, confirming my suspicions about their maturity level and intentions for coming here today.

"Look," I say under my breath to Ty, "I don't know what kind of stunt the three of you are plotting, but it's not happening. Today is too important for me."

Ty's head jerks back like he just took a punch. "We don't have any 'stunts' planned. And I know today's important. That's why I'm here. You were practically begging people to come to this thing. I'm trying to be supportive."

"No. You're trying to turn my class into a circus and embarrass me. I know you, Ty, remember? I'm not falling for your games again. We aren't in high school anymore."

"You sure about that?" Ty crosses his arms over his broad chest. "Because it doesn't seem like you can let go of anything that happened back then."

He's right about one thing, at least. I can't let it go. He got me into so much trouble, and he didn't care enough to even call afterward and make sure I was okay.

"Because you got me expelled." The words come out in a rush, three years of frustration breaking loose. "My dad almost made me move back to New York. You risked my future for a stupid prank, and now you expect me to believe you're here to support me? No." I shake my head. "Fool me once..."

Ty throws his hands up in frustration. "You are never genuinely going to forgive me, are you?" There's something like hurt dancing in his eyes. Guilt slams into me like a fist, but no. There's no way Ty was genuinely being nice by showing up here today. He couldn't have been. Right?

Anger mixes with uncertainty, making me question everything I thought I knew about him. Doubt swirls in my stomach, making me feel nauseous all over again. I reach out, but before I can touch him,

Ty snatches his recipe off the counter. The paper crumples in his hand.

"Fine. I'll go. Good luck with your class." He brushes past me, storming up the center aisle and out the doors.

A hush falls over the room, and the buzzing of the fluorescent lights overhead is suddenly loud. Crap.

I let myself get so wrapped up in Ty I forgot to keep my voice down. I glance around. Sure enough, everyone is staring at me, mouths agape.

I heave a sigh laden with humiliation and something that feels an awful lot like regret and squeeze my eyes shut. When I open them, Betty and Giselle are watching me, lips turned down in twin frowns. Liv glances from me to my phone and cringes. I wish the hardwood floor would rise up and swallow me whole. Not only did this room full of our neighbors just witness my latest blowout with Ty, but it was broadcast live for the world to see. Freaking fantastic.

My watch vibrates with a notification. I look down to see my daily inspirational text from Janet.

Janet: Being the person who makes others feel included is the most beautiful thing you can be.

Talk about advice I could've used five minutes ago. It takes everything in me not to groan out loud. I do my best to plaster on a convincing smile and take my place at the front of the classroom.

Chapter 18

I flip the page of my Current Issues in Nutrition book even though I didn't absorb a single word I just read. I'm kicked back on the sofa in the pool house. It's covered in brown and orange striped upholstery and looks like something straight out of the seventies. It's cozy, though, and I could definitely use a little comfort right about now.

I rest my open book on my stomach, snatching my cell off the coffee table. I tap on the screen, opening up Instagram. Of my fifteen-thousand followers, over three thousand watched my Livestream today. Thankfully, only two hundred people had tuned in when I went full-Karen on Ty. But since anyone on the World Wide Web could turn me into a gif with a simple screen recording, I'm keeping a very close eye on it. The last thing I need is to become an online laughing stock when I submit my application for the Happy Spoons grant. Especially since my class was a hit and may have given me an actual chance at being chosen.

Everyone seemed to have a great time. I helped them all customize the recipes they brought to substitute natural ingredients.

I'm exhausted from hustling back and forth across the room to answer questions and make sure everyone's dishes turned out just right, but it was worth it. Liv got lots of video testimonials from everybody raving about how great the modified recipes tasted. She's going to combine all the clips together, so we can include them with my application.

I push the button on the side of my phone, and it fades to black. As Janet would say, I need to stop worrying about things I can't control. But if I don't keep my mind occupied, I'll start focusing on how guilty I feel over yelling at Ty today. I think he genuinely was there to support me, and I'm not sure what to do with that.

The Ty I used to know would never have gone to a cooking class without pulling some big prank to get a laugh. That Ty could've given Johnny Knoxville a run for his money. It's possible he's changed. Or maybe he just feels bad about what happened in the past, and he's trying to make it up to me. But since we haven't spoken in the past three years, I have no idea what's going through his head. Realizing I don't know who Ty is anymore breaks another piece of my heart.

Ty was my first love and such a huge part of my life. Not knowing him is like waking up one day to find out the sun didn't rise. How am I supposed to navigate the world around me without seeing how he fits into it? And, more importantly, do I even want to?

Every time I'm near Ty, my heart simultaneously leaps and plummets, turning itself into a knot I can't untangle. The chemistry between us is undeniable. I've never been as drawn to another person as I am to Ty. All the memories of the two of us together are fresh in my mind: Ty spending days helping me modify recipes, Ty dancing in the rain with me outside our prom when I said it was my dream rom-com moment, Ty kissing me under a sky of stars and lightning bugs. But all the pain of that last fight is still there too. The hurt of not hearing from him for three entire years is an ugly, raw wound that won't heal.

The air from the ceiling fan catches at the pages of my textbook, flicking them forward and making me lose my spot. I snap the book shut and toss it on the coffee table next to the plate of crumbs—all that's left of the gluten-free cookies I made earlier. I'm about to check Instagram again when the front door swings open, and Liv walks in. Her arms are laden with bags of chips and cans of sparkling water.

"You've got to put that phone away," she says, tossing me a bag of the plantain chips we ordered from Trader Joe's. "I promise you, the internet hasn't changed in the last five seconds, which I'm guessing is how long it's been since you looked."

"You don't know me." I sit up and drop my cell on the cushion beside me. "It's been at least ten seconds."

Liv plops down in one of my mismatched armchairs and slides a can of water to me. It's my favorite flavor, Limoncello.

The wicker chair lets out a groan as Liv settles into it. "So, do you want to talk about it?"

"About having a meltdown in front of half the town and hundreds of people online? Not particularly." I crack open my water and take a sip. The citrusy-sweet bubbles dance over my tongue.

Liv lifts her brow, ice-blue eyes boring into me. "I meant about Ty."

I pop a salty-sweet plantain chip in my mouth, chewing carefully and trying to delay the conversation. I don't know what to think about Ty, let alone how to talk about him. Liv isn't going to let me off the hook that easily, though. She sits watching me chew, waiting for me to say something.

I slump against the couch cushions. "I don't know, Liv. Ty took a wrecking ball to my life and left without saying goodbye. Now he's back and being nice to me. What am I supposed to do with that?"

Liv bobs her head, nodding slowly. "I get that. And you do not have to forgive him if you aren't ready to. I just think you two should talk. Otherwise, you're stuck wondering what he's thinking and assuming the worst until you both look like jackasses on the internet."

"Thanks a lot," I grumble, but I have to admit she has a point. I've been waiting years for Ty to initiate a conversation, which hasn't exactly worked out well for me. And while I still think he should be the one to come and talk to me, I'm not doing myself any favors by being stubborn. We need to clear the air between us once and for all.

I sigh. "Maybe you're right."

Liv grins, opening a bag of Doritos and scooping out a handful. "Duh. I'm always right."

"Don't get carried away." I take another gulp of sparkling water. "Now, can we please talk about something other than the carnage of my former love life? What's going on in yours?"

"In my love life?" Liv scoffs. "Who has time for that?"

Being voted president of her sorority comes with a lot of responsibilities. I know Liv's on the phone with her sorority sisters every night, prepping for the upcoming semester. But she's been making an effort to spend as much time as possible with Betty and me this summer. It's probably the last one we'll all get to have together. Next year, she'll be off in New York, completing her residency.

I'm about to ask her how it's going when a cringe-inducing wail screeches through the open windows like a banshee's mating call.

Liv claps her hands over her ears. "What in the love of Liam Hemsworth is that?"

"Not again." I jump from the couch and rush to the windows, slamming them shut. Gary's back deck is directly on the other side of the fence from the pool house. He's been out there, practicing his rendition of 'I Don't Want To Miss A Thing' by Aerosmith every day this week.

I whirl around to face Liv. We exchange a look and collapse into a fit of giggles. With the windows shut, Gary's voice is muffled, but we can still hear it when he goes for a high note and misses. His voice cracks, echoing through the neighborhood. I'm laughing so hard I'm bent over at the waist, clutching my stomach. Liv's wheezing.

"Please, tell me he's performing that for karaoke night and that we'll be allowed to video it," she says between bursts of laughter. "My sorority sisters never believe me when I tell them how wacky this town is. I need proof."

I swipe at a tear leaking from the corner of my eye. "If you want to subject them to that torture, that's on you." I walk back over to the sofa, accidentally bumping the clipboard on the edge of my coffee table. It clatters to the floor.

"So, who won anyway?" Liv picks up the board, examining the pages. They stick out at odd, stiff angles from being dropped in the puddle.

I groan. "No idea. The ink ran so badly, I can't tell which movie people were even voting for."

"Are you going to make everyone vote again?" The pages crinkle as Liv flips through them.

I shake my head. "I think Ty and I scared enough people out of coming to movie night already."

"Good point." Liv bites into a chip. "You two clearly can't handle the responsibility. You need an impartial third party to do it."

I wince as Gary hits the bridge of the song. "Any suggestions?" I raise my voice to be heard over the cacophony.

"Mom and I can do it during the kickball game tonight." Liv opens a can of sparkling water and sips before wrinkling her nose and setting it down on the coffee table. Water doesn't meet Liv's minimum sugar requirement. I'm surprised she even tried it.

I snort. "Right. And the two of you are supposed to be impartial?"

Liv shrugs. "Well, we're slightly less partial anyway."

Gary croons the final note, his voice echoing through the room.

"It's fine by me if you can convince Ty." My eyes drop to the tile floor. Just saying his name makes my heart twinge with guilt.

Liv leans forward, elbows resting on her knees. "Okay, but for real. You two need to talk. Soon."

"We'll see." I frown, but I reach for my phone as Gary starts again from the beginning. I seriously need to invest in a pair of earmuffs.

I go to my contact list and scroll to Ty's name, something I haven't done in years. His picture is a selfie I took of the two of us down by the lake. We're both smiling hugely, looking young and head-over-heels in love. Seeing it stings like tugging on a t-shirt when your shoulders are sunburned. I hit the message button, trying not to look at the photo. Before I can change my mind, I type out the most honest text I can muster.

Me: I'm sorry. Seeing you again has just brought back a lot of old feelings. I was way out of line today. Thank you for trying to be there for me.

I shove the phone under a couch cushion, so I won't be tempted to watch for his response. Liv and I spend the afternoon typing up and printing new movie ballots and getting ready for the kickball game. I interrupt Gary's recital long enough to double-check that he knows what time to be at the field since he's refereeing. I also call Giselle to see if she needs any help with the corndogs the students from the high school will be passing out during the game, which she doesn't.

After Betty gets home from her lunch date, we get decked out in blue t-shirts. Liv refuses to change out of her black maxi dress, but she does tie a blue bandana around her wrist like a bracelet. The entire town dresses in either red or blue for the game. We never know who will show up in what color or which team they'll be on. It's, admittedly, an imperfect system. But since almost everyone picks the same colors every year, it's more predictable than you'd think. The three of us never actually play kickball, but we love cheering on—or, in Betty's case, heckling—the players from the stands.

Before I know it, it's time to leave for the game, and Ty still hasn't texted me back.

Chapter 19

The score is tied. The bases are loaded. There's one out, and I'm sitting in the dugout, bored to death. I had absolutely no intention of ever playing kickball—or any other sport, for that matter. I might be able to measure a precise teaspoon of cinnamon using only my eyes and the palm of my hand, but that's the extent of my coordination.

When the players were getting ready to take the field, the blue team came up a player short. Kallie Peters was supposed to play second base but said she was too sunburned to participate. She claimed she spent the day out waterskiing at the lake. But since Kallie's only marginally more athletically inclined than I am, it's more likely she stayed in the tanning bed at her mom's salon too long.

After Kallie bailed, the blue team was left scrambling to find another player. Ty started hinting that anyone who really cared about the town and the success of the festival would step up. He may not have been looking at me when he said it, but I knew his words were aimed at me. I wasn't about to let him think he cares more about

Rosedale than I do. So I crumbled like a cookie made with coconut flour and volunteered. That's the closest we've come to speaking to each other all night. He never responded to my text, and I don't know where that leaves us.

He's on the red team, naturally. And I can't keep myself from glancing over to where he's playing first base. I feel so guilty about kicking him out of my class. I can't stop thinking about whether or not he's mad at me.

Admittedly, my distraction may also have something to do with the fact that Ty looks exceptionally good tonight. He's wearing those old, faded blue jeans really well. I thought I caught him staring at me earlier, too. But he looked away before I could be sure. It was probably just me projecting my own fixation. I peek over at him again, but he's laser-focused on Chance, who's up to kick.

Get it together, Quinn. I toe at a loose bit of gravel in front of the bench and watch insects swarm in the giant field lights. Life will be so much easier when Ty goes back to California, but Liv's right about us needing to talk. I want to resolve everything that happened between us before he disappears again. If he'll even speak to me, that is.

Kelvin's pitching, and he lobs the ball toward Chance, who boots it full-force. It flies into the air. Applause erupts from the bleachers but dies off quickly as the ball curves toward the crowd in a foul.

Ty's dad, Marco, easily catches it. He throws it to Gary, who's standing behind home plate with an umpire's mask strapped to his face that makes his hair stick up at the back. Lisa, Francie, and Gianna are sitting next to Marco, but Lucia is MIA. This is the fourth town event she's missed this week. It isn't like her. If Marco's here, the restaurant can't be struggling. I hope the two of them aren't getting divorced or something. Marco and Lucia have always been my idea of happily ever after. You can practically feel the love radiating between them when they're together. It would break my heart if they split up.

There's a groan from the crowd, and I turn my attention back to the game. Chance must have gotten a strike because he kicks the dirt in frustration, sending a cloud of dust swirling into the air.

"Hey there, Slugger." Jenny Jenkins hurries over, plopping down beside me. "You're up next. You ready?"

I glance down the bench at the other players, hoping someone will volunteer to take my place. Al's on my other side, playing Candy Crush on his phone. Amala Reddy's next to him, but she seems to be intentionally avoiding making eye contact with me. That probably has more to do with the rain gutter regatta than her not wanting to play kickball, though. Giselle's also standing in the dugout, but she's busy yelling at one of the kids who's supposed to be passing out her corndogs and keeps eating them instead.

I suppress a sigh and try to force a smile for Jenny. "Ready as I'll ever be."

"Good girl." Jenny pats my shoulder, then she reaches for the cardigan around her waist. "Do you want to borrow this? I'd hate for you to catch a cold or something."

I blink at her. "Jenny, it's eight-nine degrees out here."

"Oh, right." She laughs, waving a hand. "I know you're sensitive, so I thought I'd offer."

My smile turns leaden, but I fight to keep it in place. "Mhmm. Thanks."

The crowd moans again, and Chance lets out a string of curse words, stomping back to the dugout and flopping down at the end of our bench.

"You're up!" Jenny places a hand on my elbow like I'm a ninety-year-old woman she has to help to her feet. "That's two outs for us, and we're still tied, so the team's counting on you. But, you know, no pressure!" She escorts me all the way to home plate as though she's worried I won't be able to make it there on my own.

I bite the inside of my cheek to keep from snapping at her and swivel my eyes toward the bleachers where Liv and Betty are making everyone vote for the movie again. I catch Betty's eye. She glances at Jenny and smacks her palm against her forehead.

I shake my head and turn my attention to the pitcher's mound, where Kelvin grins at me. Clearly, he thinks he's got this one in the bag. I don't disagree with him. Stupid sports. Who actually thinks this is fun?

He bounces the red rubber ball once before winding his arm back and hurling it at me. I swear that thing barrels toward me, going eighty miles an hour. I squeal, squeezing my eyes shut and guarding my face with my hands. I kick my leg out unseeingly and feel the ball zoom past.

"Swing and a miss!" Gary shouts so loudly from behind me it makes me jump. A few people chuckle in the stands. My eyes automatically dart over to Ty. I'm sure he's loving every second of watching me embarrass myself. But to my surprise, he's staring at the ground, hands on his hips.

"Say it a little louder, Gary," I grumble. "There might be someone in the back row who didn't hear you."

"Nope," Gary says. "I've spent hours practicing so that I can amplify my voice to the exact right decibel level. Everyone on this field can hear every word I say."

"Well, that's great." I glare at Kelvin, whose shoulders are shaking with laughter as he winds up again.

I force myself to keep my eyes open this time, but I'm still probably more surprised than anyone when my foot connects. For a second, I stand there, frozen in shock. The ball zooms past Kelvin and out toward the fence.

"Run, Quinn!" Jenny screams from the sidelines. "If you can, I mean. I'll be your pinch-runner if you need me to."

I roll my eyes and take off, running toward first base. My tennis shoes kick up dirt, and my teeth clatter as I run full-out toward Ty. He motions for Evan Harper to throw him the ball from right field.

Oh, heck no. I might feel bad for yelling at Ty earlier, but I'm not about to let him get me out. I sprint with everything I've got. From the corner of my eye, I see Evan launch the ball through the air. It hurtles at Ty as I race forward.

My sneaker kisses the base just as Ty's hands clap around the ball. He spins to try and tag me. One of his arms wraps around me, palm spread across the small of my back. His other hand gently pushes the ball against my stomach, holding me against him.

And just like that, I'm transported to three years ago—the last time Ty had his arms wrapped around me like this. Lying in the back of his truck in a field of sunflowers, watching fireflies dance through the air as the sun set behind us. We were so tangled up in one another. So in love. It was magic and joy and this feeling of utter rightness that I can't explain.

The energy between us shifts, and I can't help but wonder if Ty's remembering the same thing. Chest heaving, I stare up at him, trying to catch my breath. You wouldn't think it would be possible to get lost in a town as small as Rosedale. But I'm going to need a freaking roadmap to find my way out of his eyes. I'd almost forgotten how it feels to be caught up in him. I'm having a hard time remembering why I'd ever want to be anywhere else.

"Safe!" Gary's voice booms over the field, clear as a bell. I'm still all kinds of tangled up in Ty, though, and he doesn't seem to be in any hurry to let me go, either.

"Nice kick." Ty's gaze flickers between my eyes.

"Thanks." My voice comes out on a breath.

Ty's eyes drift down to my lips and linger, making everything inside me turn to goo. The energy zapping between us is lightning, electric and hot.

"Um, guys? We're gonna need this." Kelvin walks up behind Ty and snatches the ball from his hands.

"Right. Sorry." Ty drops his arms and steps away from me, clearing his throat.

I'm vaguely aware of people screaming Giselle's name from the stands, and I make myself turn and watch as she takes her place at home plate. My heart hums louder than the insects that flit through the thick summer air. I can't focus on anything, let alone the game.

Ty's standing behind my shoulder, less than a foot away. I've never been more aware of another human being in my life. The air between us is so palpable Ty might as well be touching me.

"I got your text. We need to talk, Quinn." Ty's voice rumbles through me. Hearing my name on his lips shatters any illusions I had that I was over him. What I'm feeling goes beyond attraction. It's more than the echoes of old feelings from when we were together. Having him come back to town has twisted me inside out. I may have achieved a lot of things in the past few years, but getting over Ty is not one of them.

I'm so overwhelmed by everything I'm feeling, my hands are trembling against my thighs. Dragging in a wobbly breath, I inhale the smell of grass, and corndogs, and something distinctly summer. Kelvin launches the ball toward Giselle.

I want to tell Ty I'm sorry again. To ask him if being apart has torn his heart into a million pieces like it's done to mine. But before I can calm my frantic mind enough to speak, Giselle's foot slams into the ball. It soars into the air, over Kelvin's head, and far out into left field. I'm still reeling from all the emotions thrumming through my system. It takes me a second to realize I need to run again.

"Go, Quinn!" Giselle screams as she sprints toward me.

I glance back at Ty long enough to see his eyes glued to me before I take off running. Giselle's hot on my heels as I round the bases. It's like someone's put me on autopilot. My legs are pumping, but my mind and heart are on another planet altogether, one where Ty and I exist all alone.

Somehow, I cross home base in front of Giselle, and Gary thunderously proclaims our team the winner. I'm swarmed by a sea of blue T-shirts. Everyone is cheering and hooting, and I'm getting a lot of slaps on the back that I'm not sure I deserve. All the while, my eyes are like heat-seeking missiles, searching for Ty in the crowd.

"I cannot believe you actually kicked the ball." Liv runs up and crushes me in a hug.

"I can't believe you didn't kick Jenny," Betty says, dropping her voice and glancing over her shoulder to make sure Jenny isn't within earshot.

"No kidding." I try to make my voice sound normal even though it feels like the Earth has suddenly started rotating backward.

"Good game," Ty says from behind me. I turn to see him holding out his hand for a high-five. His lips are curled in a small smile that sends my stomach cartwheeling.

"You too." I slap his hand. As our skin makes contact, Ty threads his fingers through mine. Our hands drop, and he holds on for just a second before letting go. "So, we're going to talk later, right?"

"Definitely." I catch myself staring at his mouth and force my eyes up to his.

Ty nods. "Have a good night," he says to Betty and Liv, giving me one last lingering smile before striding off toward his truck. I watch him walk away, heart in my throat.

"I'm sorry. Is the field on fire?" Betty asks.

"What?" I whirl around.

Liv shoots me a wicked grin. "Well, with all those sparks flying between you two, we were sure something was about to go up in flames."

There's no point denying the all-out blaze that ignites between Ty and me whenever we're together. Even Gary, Captain Oblivious, had to have noticed the chemistry sizzling between us out there.

I groan, pressing a hand over my face. My hormones were just on display for the entire town. This one's going in my most embarrassing moments hall of fame, which, thanks to Ty, is extensive.

Betty puts an arm around my shoulders and steers me toward the parking lot. "Come on, Juliette. Let's get you home. I'm pretty sure there's a balcony with your name on it."

Chapter 20

I sit on a stool in the empty classroom, using my LightRoom App to edit the photo of the matcha cookies I just made. I dial up the exposure to make the white plate they're displayed on brighter. Then I adjust the color so it saturates the green of the cookies. Upping the brightness and lowering the clarity gives the picture that light, airy vibe that's so big on Instagram. The cookies in the photograph look even more mouth-watering than in real life. It's too bad no one was interested in coming to learn how to make them.

Everyone seemed so enthusiastic after my last class. I was sure at least a few of them would show up today. But Giselle's face is the only one I've seen all morning. She gave me a pep talk when I almost broke down in tears over the non-existent turnout. She thinks the picture of the green cookies we included on this week's calendar may have scared people away.

"Even Gary would get nervous about eating a green dessert," she said.

My matcha cookies are amazing. They're one of my favorite things I make, but I can see her point. To people unfamiliar with matcha powder, they probably resemble something that came out of the wrong end of the Grinch.

The drone of power tools emanates from behind the drop cloth that divides the classroom from the new addition. Al and his team are hard at work this morning.

I sigh and glance over. I can just make out the shadows moving around behind the tarp. It's impossible to distinguish one silhouette from the next. I'm not sure if Ty's over there this morning, but the possibility he could be so close has my heart spinning like a pinwheel.

I'm dying to talk to him, to find out if he's still as caught up in me as I am in him. There's no denying I want Ty as much as ever, but I can't ignore the resentment simmering under the surface, which the past three years of total silence have only made worse. I'm never sure which emotion will win out when I'm near him. I go from wanting to jump his bones to screaming at him in less time than it takes for a heart to beat. And I can't shake the feeling that I don't even know who Ty is anymore.

Trying to distract myself, I open up Instagram and prep a post for my matcha cookies. I snatch one of them from the plate and copy over the recipe from my Notes App. I add a snazzy caption about how these cookies will make anyone not eating them turn green with envy. Judging by my empty classroom, that may be a bit of an over-exaggeration.

I take a big bite at the same moment the drop cloth pulls backward, and Ty steps into the room. His eyes sweep the deserted cooking stations before settling on mine. My cheeks are already crammed with cookie, but there's still room for them to fill with heat. It's humiliating to have Ty find me here alone, stuffing my face when no one bothered to show up for my class.

"Hi." Ty shoves his hands in the pockets of his sawdust-covered jeans and walks toward me.

I point a finger at my full mouth in explanation for my lack of response. Ty chuckles, nodding as I chew...and chew...and chew. I swear, it's never taken me this long to eat anything in my life. But any moisture in my mouth vanished the second I saw Ty's face.

Grabbing my Stanley cup, I take a glug and finally, wash down the crumbs."Hi." Is all I can think to say. Seriously? Could I be more awkward?

Ty reaches for one of the cookies, taking a bite without the slightest bit of hesitation, which is something I always loved about him. No matter how off-the-wall the recipes I created were, he was always right there with me when it was time to try them.

His eyes light up. "These are good. What are they?"

"Matcha green tea cookies. I'm glad you like them, at least." I glance around the vacant classroom.

Ty follows my gaze. "Did you kick everyone else out too?"

I snort out a laugh. "Just you. No one else makes me quite that mad." I'm not sure if I mean 'mad' in the angry or bananas sense of the word. Either way, it works.

"I'm honored." Ty shakes his head, but a grin curves the corners of his mouth. "It's their loss, anyway. These are great."

"Thanks." Nerves crackle through me, making me feel like a bowl of Rice Krispies.

The sound of Al and his crew talking and laughing drifts through the tarp while the smell of wood shavings fills the air, making me want to sneeze.

Ty clears his throat. "So how, um...how are you?"

"I'm great. Really good." I bob my head a little too enthusiastically.

"You look really good," Ty says, and my gaze snaps to his. His eyes drop, and he gestures at my phone on the counter. "And, uh, your cooking stuff seems to be going well. You're, like, Insta-famous now."

Heat sears up my neck, and I force myself to keep my hands in my lap instead of trying to cover my reddening skin. "You too. Look good, I mean." There's a lump in my throat the size of Paula's festival binder. I try to swallow it down.

"Yeah. I knew what you meant." Ty's eyes keep flicking away from me like he's uncomfortable as I am.

All those scenes in rom-coms where the characters shove everything off the desk and just go to town are starting to make a lot of sense. It would be so much easier to work out all this tension that way rather than attempting to form coherent sentences.

"So, how'd the vote go?" Ty asks.

Someone pounds a hammer on the other side of the wall. "Well," I shout to be heard over the racket, "Betty and Liv managed to get everyone's vote, minus Old Man Jenkins and the Reddys. Apparently, Faris and Amala flat-out refused to participate again."

"Can't say I blame them. So, which movie won?"

"Ever After by a landslide." The hammering cuts off abruptly, making my words resonate through the room. My teeth tug at my lip. I imagined this moment feeling so different than it actually does. I had daydreams about gloating over how much better I know this town than Ty does. But now that I've won and can see the disappointed slump to Ty's shoulders, I just feel bad.

Ty shrugs, smiling in a way that seems forced. "I can't say I'm surprised. I mean, Liv and Betty weren't exactly unbiased arbiters. But I'm not about to call for another re-vote."

"Well, that's a relief. The good people of Rosedale might rise up against us if we put them through that again."

"Right." Ty scuffs his shoe against the floor, and we fall into an uncomfortable silence.

The weight of everything we aren't saying is so heavy it's making it hard to breathe. I can't take another minute of not knowing what's going through his head.

"Ty?" I ask. His eyes lock on mine, causing my pulse to skitter. "Why are you here?"

"I came to see if Giselle needs help getting the brownies and punch over to the barn for the dance tonight." His eyes skate around the room. "But it doesn't look like she's around."

We're having a dance out at the barn on the edge of town later. It's always been my favorite festival tradition, even though it's been years since I've had anyone I actually like to dance with.

I shake my head. "No. I mean, you haven't come home in years. Why now?"

"Oh." Ty shifts from foot to foot, staring at the floor. "I'm here for summer break." His tan face flushes red, and I can tell he's lying. I just can't figure out why.

I'm exhausted from spending years wondering what Ty's thinking and feeling. I've used up too much energy trying to understand why he never came to talk to me after that night, and I have no patience for his evasiveness anymore. Especially since he keeps sending me all those longing glances like he wants to come over here and reenact some of my favorite memories of the two of us together.

I'm about to call him out and demand he be honest when the tarp flips open again, and Giselle strides into the room. The heels of her open-toed booties clack against the hardwood floor.

"Al said you were over here," she says to Ty. "Do you want to help me load the brownies into my car for the dance tonight?"

Ty nods, looking relieved to have a change of subject. "Yeah, I actually just came over to see if you needed a hand."

"Uh-huh." Giselle glances between us, clearly not believing what he's saying any more than I do. But she doesn't comment on it. "The brownies are on the racks in the refrigerators if you want to start loading them."

"Sure. I'll be right there," Ty says as she walks out the door to where her BMW's parked at the curb. She climbs into the front seat and presses a button, lifting the hatch.

Ty turns back to me, raking a hand through his hair. "Look, I know we still need to talk, just...later. When we won't be interrupted?"

I raise my eyebrows. "And you'll tell me everything?"

"I'll tell you as much as I can."

I sigh. The last thing I need is more half-truths from him.

"Please, Quinn." His voice is so earnest it makes me melt like the butter on Betty's popcorn.

"Okay," I say, hoping I don't regret this later.

"Okay." Ty grins. "I'll see you at the barn tonight."

I try to match his enthusiasm, but mostly all I feel is anxiety over our impending conversation. "See you tonight."

Ty walks toward the refrigerators, but he stops. "Oh, and Quinn?"

"Yeah?"

"Save me a dance?"

My heart trips over itself like I'm a heroine in a Jane Austen novel when having a guy ask you to dance was akin to a marriage proposal. Part of me wants to tell Ty to go jump in the lake, but a much bigger part wants nothing more than to be in his arms again.

Apparently, there aren't any words remaining in my vocabulary after getting locked in another tug-of-war with my own emotions, though. All I can do is nod.

Ty smiles, and his gaze skims over my face, snagging on my mouth. His eyes fill with unmistakable wanting, leaving me breathless. Then he turns and hurries after Giselle.

I sincerely hope she has a defibrillator because, after that look, I am completely and perfectly and incandescently dead.

Chapter 21

I pull Betty's Prius into the parking lot. Fields of sunflowers surround the barn, glowing in the rays of the setting sun. Warm, golden light spills out the barn doors and across the asphalt. The twangy melody of a country song fills the night air. Parking, I do a quick check of my makeup in the rearview. I swipe a finger under my eyes to get rid of any mascara smudges and apply another layer of lipgloss. Then I toss the keys and tube of gloss in my clutch and scramble out of the car. I'm unsurprisingly late, but this time I had a good reason.

After my sorry excuse for a class this morning, I stopped by to make sure everything was ready for the dance. The barn hasn't been home to any farm animals in years. The owners realized long ago that it was more lucrative to use the rustic, old building to host events like weddings, birthday parties, and the annual Founder's Festival Dance.

By the time I arrived, Ty and Giselle already had the punch and brownies chilling in the kitchen's refrigerators. The event staff had lined the dance floor with strategically stacked bales of straw, which they used to hold up the poles for the twinkle lights, zig-zagging above the room.

I sat down on one of the bales to call Liv and make sure she and Betty would be back in time for the dance. They drove over to the neighboring town of River Hollow, to hit up the diner there for Waffle Wednesday. By the time Liv confirmed they'd be here, my legs had begun to itch. When I hung up and checked my calves, they were covered in red, angry welts. Apparently, straw is yet another item to add to my ever-growing list of things I react to.

It took two showers, a lot of Benadryl cream, and a few ice packs to get my skin to calm down. By the time I was dressed and hive-free, the dance had already started.

I slam the car door behind me and speed walk across the lot. Even though I was here earlier, the sight of the dance floor takes my breath away. All lit up, the place is magical. It's like the country version of A Midsummer's Night Dream. The giant beams of the ceiling glow in the lights. The worn wood flooring reverberates with the footsteps of couples swaying together. The earthy scent of dried grass and lavender lingers in the air. The atmosphere is enchanting, as though the joy in the room is contagious.

I spot Giselle at the refreshment table and cut a path over to her. Rows of brownies are set out on napkins on one side of the table. A large punch bowl sits on the other, which Giselle's keeping a careful eye on. Her gaze keeps flicking from the bowl to Chance, who's standing just feet away, watching the dancers. Smart woman. Sure as a football in an end zone, that punch would be spiked if Chance was left alone with it.

"Hey," I say to Giselle. "What can I help with?"

I texted her earlier, so she knows why I'm late, but I still feel bad.

Giselle tears her eyes away from Chance to examine me. She takes in my off-white, lace mini dress. It has bell sleeves, and I've matched it with an old pair of Betty's cowgirl boots. Liv curled my hair in wild waves while I lathered up in Benadryl cream. I can never style the messy look myself. My need for precision only allows me to curl it in neat rolls. I do love the full, chaotic way it looks tonight, though. Like I'm a girl who doesn't have the weight of chronic illness and mounting medical expenses resting on her shoulders.

"You look beautiful," Giselle says. "How are you feeling?"

"Much better. Sorry I'm late. I was planning to help with all of this." I gesture at the table laden with goodies.

"Don't worry about it." Giselle flaps a dismissive hand. "You're young. You should be out there dancing. Not hanging out over here with this oldie moldy."

"You're hardly old," I say, even though I'm not sure how old Giselle is. She's one of those people who are timeless. She could pass for anything between twenty-nine and forty-five.

I glance around as the deep voice of Kane Brown floods the room. Aaron Martinez and Pete Winchester sway together in the corner of the dance floor. Kelvin is spinning Liv around and around in circles. She's cackling with laughter as she wobbles in her high-heeled boots. Betty's arms are around Al's shoulders, and she's beaming up at him. Interesting.

Betty never brings men home, so I've only seen her look at someone like that one other time. And that was only because Liv and I accidentally caught her making out with the guy in the driveway when he dropped her off after their date. I have to admit, Al is pretty dashing tonight. He's traded his usual t-shirt for a crisp button-down, and his salt-and-pepper hair's been combed back.

I can't find the one face I'm searching for in the sea of people, though. I haven't stopped thinking about Ty asking me to save him a dance. Liv and I analyzed his words over and over again as she curled my hair. I insisted that he must have only said that to be nice since he probably felt bad after finding me sitting alone in my classroom. Liv said I was being stupid and that it was obvious Ty's still into me.

I'm not sure which explanation I want to be true more. On the one hand, admitting I'm still into Ty is the understatement of the century. That boy sets my soul on fire anytime he comes near me. But I don't know if I'm ready to go there again. Not when I still don't understand how he could have left without a goodbye or why he's back now.

My clutch vibrates, and I fish out my phone. The screen glows with my daily Janet text.

Janet: Take the risk or lose the chance.

I think the message is meant to give me a boost of inspiration about the Happy Spoons Grant. But right now, dancing with Ty feels like the bigger risk. The idea of being that close to him has me tangled up in more knots than Rapunzel's hair.

"Have you seen Ty?" I ask Giselle, trying to play it cool like I couldn't care less. I must fail, though, because she gives me a sideways smirk, eyes sparkling suggestively.

"Yeah, I've seen him. He's looking very handsome too." She watches me carefully, gauging my reaction.

"Good for him." I tuck my phone back in my bag and run a hand through my hair, avoiding her eyes. I know Giselle's interested in my love life because she cares about me. But I'm not ready for the whole town to be up in my business with Ty, especially when I have no idea where we stand.

"Oh, hey. Isn't that him over—" Giselle cuts off abruptly. She bites her lower lip as though she'd like to unsay those words. Her eyes dart over to me, and there's something like pity there. My stomach bottoms out.

I turn my gaze to the part of the dance floor she was looking at, and sure enough, there's Ty. Giselle wasn't wrong about how handsome he is. He's wearing a blue and tan plaid shirt tucked into a pair of faded jeans. His belt is the same shade as the boots I know he bought the summer he worked out on the Jones's ranch. He also seems very preoccupied.

Kallie Baker's arms are around him. Her fingers trace the fine hairs at the base of his neck as they move to the music. My own fingers tingle, remembering how it felt to touch him like that. I can only see Ty's back, but Kallie's grinning up at him with stars in her eyes. He says something, and she bursts out laughing before looping her arms more tightly together, pulling him closer.

My eyes flood with unshed tears, and I fight to swallow them down. I don't know what I expected from tonight. For us to finally sort through the wreckage of our former love life and start building something new? For Ty to say he still wants to be with me? I'm not even sure I want those things. But whatever I thought would happen, it never crossed my mind that I'd find him here, dancing with another girl like she's...well, like she's me from three years ago.

My chest constricts, and it's getting hard to breathe. "Giselle, I, uh, left something in my car. I'll be right back."

"Okay, sweetheart. Take your time." Giselle's voice is filled with sympathy. It undoes me. A single tear breaks free, trickling down my cheek.

I train my eyes on the distressed planks of the floor and hustle toward the door. I can't help peeking over at Ty and Kallie one last time as I rush past them. When I do, Ty's staring right at me. He takes in my expression, and his smile drops, forehead creasing with worry.

I snap my gaze forward and practically run out the door. I barely make it outside before the tears start to fall in earnest.

Chapter 22

I lean against the side of the barn, breathing in the tangy scent of freshly-cut hay and trying to slow the hammering of my fragmented heart. I press my palm against my chest, forcing myself to focus on the steady rise and fall as I stare up at the sea of stars, blinking back tears.

The sunflowers in the field rustle in the faint breeze, and fireflies dance through the air. They remind me of all the times Ty and I sat out here watching them from the bed of his pickup truck before getting lost in each other. I never felt safer or more whole than I did on those nights we spent together. But thinking about it now only makes the chasm in my heart crack wider.

The pain of watching Ty in there with Kallie sears through me again. He's never posted any photos on social media to make me think he was with anyone new. And while I always assumed he'd move on eventually, I always envisioned him falling for some girl out in California. Some anonymous person I'd never have to see in a place where my memories with Ty feel close enough to touch.

"Quinn!"

Ty runs out the front doors of the barn and stops. His head whips back and forth, searching the parking lot. His hands drop to his sides, and his shoulders slump when he finds it empty. I can't imagine why he'd be disappointed not to find me when I'm sure Kallie's inside waiting for him.

But before I have time to puzzle it out, he turns. His gaze meets mine through the darkness, and he strides toward me without hesitation, not stopping until he's standing only inches away.

"What happened back there? Why'd you leave?" His eyes search my face like he's hoping to see the answers written there.

Maintaining eye contact with him makes the wave of emotions rolling through me swell until I'm certain they're going to drag me under and wash me away. I focus on a point over his shoulder.

"I needed some air."

"You looked upset."

I want to say something snarky to him because, of course, I'm upset. He shows up again out of the blue, acting like he still cares about me, asking me to save him a dance, turning my life upside down. And while he might not have said otherwise, I certainly didn't expect to discover I was just one of the many girls he planned to get cozy with on the dance floor.

I have no idea how to explain everything I'm feeling, though. Laying my soul bare in front of Ty when he's given me nothing but loaded glances to go off of is terrifying. So all I say is, "I'm fine."

"Don't do that." Ty scrubs an irritated hand over the back of his neck. "Don't tell me you're fine when you're not."

"What do you want me to say, Ty?" Tears sting the back of my eyes again, and I fight to keep my voice from wavering. How can he act like he knows me better than anyone and still be completely oblivious to the fact that he's stomping all over what's left of my heart?

"I want you to tell me the truth!" Ty's words echo off the barn wall, frustration bursting out of him. His head droops, and he lets out a sigh, lowering his voice. "I want—no. I need you to tell me where your mind's at. You get jealous when you see me dancing with Kallie. And you look at me like..." He trails off, and I want to interrupt, to tell him I'm not jealous. That I couldn't care less. But I can't bring myself to lie to him, not when he's standing so close and looking like his heart's in as many pieces as my own. Ty's gaze falls to the ground, and he swallows. "You look at me like you still want to be with me, and it's killing me, Quinn."

"It's killing you?" I snap because how dare he act like he's the victim here. He's the one who wouldn't listen when I told him not to pull that prank in high school. He's the one who got me arrested and left without apologizing. And he's the one who's going to leave me behind again in the fall. "You show up here like nothing's changed. Like you didn't break my heart and skip town without looking back. Meanwhile, I'm stuck here with a million memories of us I can't forget no matter how hard I try."

"You think just because I've been in California, I don't remember? I think about you—about us—all the time. I can't get you out of my head. Why do you think I haven't come home until now?"

"I wouldn't know since you haven't spoken to me in three years, Ty!" I can't keep from yelling. I'm so exasperated with him and with myself. I know I should have moved on with my life already. But no matter how hard I try, Ty's still the only person my heart wants.

"You said you never wanted to talk to me again!" Ty shouts right back.

I wince because that is one of the many things I screamed at him in the parking lot of the police station after our families came to bail us out that night. But I didn't mean it, and I thought he knew that. I slump back against the barn, the fight draining out of me. "Of course, that would be the one time you actually listened to something I said."

Surprise flickers over Ty's features, and he stands there staring at me. His throat bobs in the light of the full moon, watching us from above. In the sudden silence, the opening notes of 'Boot Scootin' Boogie' ring out, and everyone inside cheers. Someone, probably Kelvin, lets out a loud, "Yeeeeehaw!"

But I'm barely aware of anything or anyone else as Ty takes a step closer to me. He leans forward, resting his palms against the wall on either side of my head. He's so close it makes my blood race. Everything in me thrums and whirls until I can hardly tell which way is up.

"Quinn, are you telling me you didn't want to break up?" Ty's gaze darts between my eyes. His lips are drawn in a hard line, and deep grooves are etched across his forehead. I've never seen him look more serious, like my answer has the power to shift the axis of his entire world.

"Of course I didn't, you idiot." I shake my head. "I spent the entire summer waiting for you to come back to me, but you just...left."

"You told me to leave you alone. I thought I was respecting our wishes. It was the hardest thing I've ever done. I thought moving to California would help me get over you, but it didn't. And I couldn't come back, knowing I'd see you. Knowing it would tear me apart all over again. I just—I couldn't." Ty's eyes are shining now too.

Seeing him hurting rips something open inside of me. I want to comfort him, to hold him. But I don't know if I should or if he'd even want me to. I wrap my arms protectively around my middle. "Well, you're back now. So does that mean you did it? You got over me?"

My tears are so close to spilling over. I'm sure I'm going to start crying in earnest if I look at his face for another second. I turn my head away, but Ty places a hand on my cheek, making me meet his eyes.

"Quinn, I'm not over you. I don't think I'll ever be over you."

His eyes wander down to my lips, and he swallows again.

All the wondering, hurting, and wanting I've ignored for the last three years bubble to the surface like a kettle ready to boil. It's too much to keep inside anymore.

I'm not sure who moves first, but the next thing I know, my hands are cupping his face. His stubble scratches against my skin, and his fingers dig into my hips, pulling me against him. My back is flush against the barn, and Ty's lips crash into mine. It's lightning during a summer storm, burned-out embers reigniting. His kiss blazes through me, raging like wildfire, turning all my doubts about his feelings to ash.

I want Ty with all I have, all I am. Being with him is everything, and I know deep in my soul that if we crash and burn like last time, I'll never be over him, either. My heart belongs to him. It always has. Even when he makes me crazy. Even when he makes me hurt.

I twine my arms behind his neck, tugging him closer as his hands trail down my sides, leaving trails of sparks kindling beneath my dress. My lips part, deepening our kiss. Ty grips my hips, lifting me easily. I gasp, wrapping my legs around his waist as warmth fills me. His mouth finds mine again, and our lips move together as my fingers tangle in his hair.

Ty's heart pounds against mine, and I can't fathom why we've spent all these years away from each other when we could've been doing this all along.

White light spills out the doors, illuminating the shadows, and we startle apart. The music has stopped, and people are calling out their goodbyes. The dance is over, and someone must have turned on the bright overhead lights inside.

Slowly, Ty sets me on my feet. My skirt has ridden up, and I tug it down but don't move away from him. I hate the idea of being separated again, even if it's only by inches. He leans his forehead against mine like he's not ready to let go of me yet, either. Our breaths entwine as we struggle to calm our racing hearts.

Ty reaches up and tucks my hair behind my ear. His thumb caresses the skin of my cheek, which heats under his touch. He releases a heavy breath, taking a step back as people start flooding out of the barn and into the parking lot.

"We should probably get in there and help Giselle clean up." Ty runs a hand through his hair. My eyes land on his kiss-swollen lips, and it takes all my self-control not to launch myself at him again.

"We should." My voice is embarrassingly breathy, and I clear my throat.

Ty starts to walk back inside. He reaches back like he wants me to take his hand. Then he glances over at the parking lot and lets it fall.

"Ty," I say, and he turns back to me. "We still need to talk." That kiss might've obliterated any uncertainty about how Ty and I feel about each other, but we still have issues we need to work through. And

I've got to know where this thing is going. The idea that we could be done again at the end of the summer makes everything in me ache.

Ty nods. "Tonight? I can come by your place."

"Okay." A smile slips over my lips. Knowing I'll get to see him again so soon, get to touch him. It lights me up like all those fireflies in the field behind us.

"Okay." Ty winks. He pivots on the heel of his boot and walks away, leaving me in a puddle on the gravel.

Chapter 23

I stare in the mirror, brushing my teeth for the second time in the last twenty minutes. I'm not worried about the state of my breath. But if I don't keep my hands busy, I might legit explode.

My hair's still down in messy curls, and I'm wearing a pair of athletic shorts with an old Fall Out Boy T-shirt of Ty's that I never gave back to him. I appear calm, cool, and casual—the exact opposite of how I feel.

Every time I think about that kiss outside the barn, my stomach turns itself inside out. Ty didn't specify what time he was coming over. The idea that he could show up at any second has anticipation and nervousness crackling through me. How is someone supposed to act after their ex-boyfriend confesses he still has feelings for them and then proceeds to kiss the life out of them?

It was all I could do to get through the clean-up after the dance. The atmosphere between Ty and me was so charged, Giselle's lucky she wasn't electrocuted in the crossfire. Ty kept finding ways to touch me. Brushing his fingers against mine as he handed me a garbage bag. Setting his hand on the small of my back when he thought no one was looking. Turning me into a weak-kneed mess.

If I survive an entire conversation with him, it'll be a miracle. I groan, shutting off the sink and tossing my toothbrush in the holder. I could really use one of Janet's motivational texts right about now.

My bare feet pad against the tile floor, which is still warm even though the sun set hours ago. I walk over to the windows, pushing them open to let in some air.

A pickup I'd recognize anywhere pulls into the driveway. Headlights flood the pool house, and tires grind against gravel as Ty parks. He might as well have put my heart into park, too, because it's definitely stopped beating. The hinges of Ty's door squeak as he gets out. It takes all my self-control to keep from running to the door.

I've spent so much time thinking about all the things that went wrong between us. But now that he's here, I'm having a hard time remembering a single one. I don't know how I'll even be able to speak with the feel of his kiss so fresh on my lips.

I shimmy my shoulders, trying to shake off the anxiety, and tug open the door. Ty's fist is raised like he was about to knock, but he isn't empty-handed. He's holding the most enormous bouquet of sunflowers I've ever seen.

I try to fight the dopey smile spreading across my face and fail. Ty brought me those same flowers so many times when we were together. I shouldn't be surprised he remembered they're my favorite. But I am. Surprised and incredibly impressed.

"They're a couple years late," Ty says. "But, I hope you'll accept these as my official apology for being the world's biggest idiot."

I take the flowers from him, too touched to say anything but "Come on in, California boy."

"That nickname's going to stick, isn't it?" Ty frowns, but there's a grin in the way his eyes crinkle.

"Afraid so." I shrug.

"Guess I'll have to get used to it then." Ty's gaze travels over my body, turning me into a puddle of goop on the tile. "Nice shirt," he says appreciatively as he walks past me into the room.

I release a wobbly breath, pushing the door shut and watching Ty as he takes in the outdated kitchen and eclectic furniture of the living room. He nods. "This place is great. Very cozy."

"It's a work in progress," I say, grabbing a vase from under the sink and filling it with water.

"I love it." Ty flops down on the worn cushions of my couch. Hearing him compliment my home makes me all floaty, like he's admiring a part of me and not just the room.

"Thanks." I place the sunflowers on the counter and sit on the sofa. I fold in one leg, so I can face him. "So..." I say, letting myself really look at Ty. I don't glance away, not even when his beautiful face makes my heart twinge. His warm eyes are lined with dark lashes, and he's got one of those mouths that's always on the verge of a smile. To look at Ty is to feel sunshine on your skin. He's everything bright and fun. He's my own personal brand of fairytale.

"So..." Ty angles his body toward mine. He takes my hands; his thumbs draw circles over my knuckles. He's apparently decided to take the rip-off-the-bandaid approach to this conversation. He takes a breath and says, "Quinn, I'm so sorry about everything that happened between us. I was young and stupid. We were getting so serious so fast." His eyes drop to our joined hands, and he swallows. "I don't think I was ready for us, but I still can't believe I risked everything we had for a prank. We were great together. Like, hall-of-fame status." He laughs, but his voice is thick with emotion. "I missed us every single day I was gone. I missed you."

My eyes burn. It doesn't bode well for the rest of the night if I'm already tearing up. I blink and try to pull myself together. "I missed us too, Ty. I know I overreacted that night. But I'd just gotten my life and my condition under control, and it felt like you didn't care that you were jeopardizing my future."

Ty squeezes his eyes shut. "You were so mad, and I got defensive when I should've been listening. Should've been begging you for your forgiveness. But believe me, I cared. When you said you never wanted to speak to me again, it destroyed me, Quinn. I'd never loved anyone the way I loved you. The idea that you could write me off like that, it broke every piece of me."

Hearing him say that word, 'loved,' it undoes me. I bite my lip to keep it from wobbling. "I didn't mean it. I was just upset and scared. I regretted every word I said before we even drove out of the parking lot. But I thought you'd come and apologize like always, and we'd put the pieces back together." My fingers tremble as I pull my hand from his and trace the features of his face: his cheekbones, his lips. "I could never write you off, Ty. Never."

Ty reaches up, placing his hand over mine. Being here with all our barricades down is heart-stingingly familiar. I haven't felt a rush like this since before he walked away from me. It's like coming up for air after drowning. I can't imagine how I've survived this long without this connection.

Ty's hands move to my shoulders, skimming down my arms. "Where do we go from here?"

"I'm not sure. I mean, you're leaving again in a couple months, right?" I let my hand drop to my lap. Because no matter how good—how right—it feels to be with him, I can't let myself get wrapped up in us, knowing we have an expiration date.

Ty clears his throat. "I'm, uh, not going back to school in the fall."

I slump back against the sofa, surprise draining the strength from my muscles. Going to UCLA was Ty's dream for as long as I've known him. His dad got his MBA there. Marco always made California sound like this sunny, magical adventure. I would have wanted to go myself if I could afford the tuition or the student loans.

In a town as small as Rosedale, there's no way I wouldn't have heard about it if Ty had graduated early, and I can't fathom the idea of him quitting. Not after the hoops I'm sure he had to jump through to keep UCLA from revoking his admission offer after we got suspended. We weren't speaking at the time, so I don't know all the details. But Liv mentioned him doing a lot of community service and writing letters to the school, disclosing what happened and how he'd grown from the experience.

"What are you talking about? You aren't dropping out."

"No." Ty shakes his head adamantly, but he's not making eye contact with me. "I'm doing my courses online this semester, so I can be home."

Warning bells go off in my mind. It isn't like Ty's just taking general classes anymore. And I doubt UCLA lets students randomly do all their studies from home during their senior year. "Why would they let you do that?"

"They allow it in certain situations." Ty still isn't meeting my eyes, and my head spins with the infinite possibilities 'certain situations' could imply.

"What kind of situations?" I lean forward, trying to force him to look at me.

"I can't talk about it." The glint in Ty's eyes is so full of pain that it steals the breath from my lungs. It kills me to see him hurting. My gut instinct is to do anything to protect him from that pain, to make him smile again. But I can't do that at the risk of getting my heart broken again. I can't.

"Ty..." I bury my face into my hands, kneading my forehead with my fingertips. I thought we were finally breaking through the walls we erected between us, but he's still keeping things from me.

Ty's fingers thread through mine, and he gently pulls my hands away from my face. "I'll tell you everything. I just...can't yet."

My heart's being tugged and twisted in so many different directions; it's Silly Putty in my chest. I can't decide what I'll regret more: risking getting hurt again or not giving us another shot.

"When?" I ask.

"Soon."

At my exasperated look, Ty pulls me closer to him and pushes my hair back from my face. I don't resist.

"I promise," he says. "Anything you want to know, I'll tell you the second I can. I just need you to be patient with me for a little while."

I chew the inside of my cheek. I want to trust him, but it's hard to do that when he's hiding something so obviously important. "I don't know."

"Quinn, please." Ty's voice trembles, shaking me to my core. "I'm still so..." he trails off, swallowing hard and leaving me in agony over how he was about to finish that sentence. "Please, give me another chance." Ty's words are a whisper against my skin.

My eyes flutter shut. I attempt to cling to any of the many reasons why being with Ty is a bad idea. But It's like trying to hold water in my hands. My objections slip through my fingers until all that's left is the love that still lingers despite how much time or distance we put between us.

I'm lost in a sea of feeling so intense I can't form the words to respond. I reach for Ty at the same moment he crushes me against him. My lips find his, and I pour everything I'm incapable of saying into that kiss.

Desire, fear, and the need to try again burn like live coals inside me. I climb onto his lap so I'm straddling his hips. Ty's hands tangle in my hair. His lips part mine, kissing me until I'm breathless and gasping. The back of his shirt bunches in my fists, and I tug it over his head.

My gaze travels over the defined muscles of his chest and shoulders. If this was Instagram instead of real life, I'd be convinced he'd drawn those muscles on in post. "Okay, seriously," I say, breathing hard. "What are they feeding you out in California?"

Ty chuckles, keeping his arms locked around me. "I, um—I hit the gym whenever I need to make myself stop thinking about you."

Okay, yeeeeah. If he wasn't holding me, I'd be full-on swooning on the tile.

"Well, you must think about me a lot." I trace my hands appreciatively over his pecks and down his chiseled abs.

"You have no idea." He pulls back, and there's a hint of a smirk in Ty's voice as he says, "You sure about this, new girl? You're really ready to give us another chance?"

My need for Ty has annihilated all my pretenses and left me raw and wholly honest. "I've never been so sure of anything in my life."

Ty's gaze crashes into mine, and there's no mistaking the love that remains there after all this time.

Chapter 24

- -

"You've truly outdone yourself, woman." I stare slack-jawed at Liv's laptop, which is sitting on Betty's kitchen table. Not only did she splice together the clips of everyone raving about my class, but she included screenshots of comments from my Instagram posts.

My eyes well. This. This is the reason I want to be a nutrition counselor. Helping people find joy in food despite their dietary restrictions is the greatest feeling in the world. When I was at my sickest, I spent months eating nothing but beef and a handful of vegetables. If I ate anything else, I flared up within hours. Mealtimes became something I dreaded. But after a while, my flare-ups eased. My body stabilized. Slowly, I was able to add more foods back into my diet. I'll never forget the first batch of AIP brownies I made. It was the first time I had hope that I might get to live a somewhat normal life again. And that hope, it was everything.

Helping others find that same optimism drives me to go after my dreams. Lately, it seems like there's been one obstacle after the next, trying to keep me from reaching my goal. But watching this video makes me realize I'm already making a difference. I'm just crossing my fingers that once the judges for the Happy Spoons Grant see this, they'll agree.

"Thank you," I say to Liv as a tear rolls down my cheek. I laugh, scrubbing at my face and glancing at the stainless-steel ceiling fan whirring above us. "Jeez. I'm such a baby."

"Hey, there's no crying on craft day." Betty points her glue gun at me. A blob of glue squirts out the end and plops onto the white wooden table that Betty bought at a yard sale. She sanded and re-painted it to make it look new. She frowns at the gluey splotch. It's been years since she fired up that glue gun, and the smell of burning dust and chemicals is acrid, singeing my nostrils.

"It's your daughter's fault." I shut the laptop, setting it on the counter behind me. I snatch a paper towel, swiping at the glue. All I manage to do is smear it across the table.

"Remind me why we're doing crafts again." Liv wrinkles her nose at the uneven ribbon of fabric she cut out. "The words 'craft' and 'Thursday' don't even start with the same letters. I thought that's what we were going for."

"You try thinking of a new way to celebrate each day, missy. I'm running out of alliterative activities. Besides, just because we haven't historically excelled in arts and crafts doesn't mean we can't start now. We're Kelley women. We can conquer anything."

Betty tucks a hair elastic inside a strip of neon-green polyester. She draws a line of hot glue around the edge of the fabric before folding the edges together and pinching them firmly shut. "Ta-da!"

Betty holds up her finished scrunchie with a flourish. It's lopsided, most of the fabric bunching at one end. As she waves it around, glue oozes out the seam, sticking to her fingers. Betty glances down at it and flicks her hand, trying to free it from the gooey mess. "Okay, maybe we aren't quite ready to conquer the fine art of the scrunchie."

"No kidding." Liv tosses her fabric down and leans back in her chair, taking a sip of her latte. She and Betty picked up coffee from the cart next to the park this morning and were nice enough to bring me a green tea with coconut milk.

Betty drops her scrunchie and walks over to the sink. She flips on the tap, attempting to scrub the glue from her fingers. "We can chalk this one up as a learning experience, but this isn't over. I won't surrender until I'm a certified domestic goddess."

"Whatever you say, Martha Stewart." Liv starts gathering up the scrunchie supplies scattered across the table. "Don't you need to get ready for your date?"

"Date?" I ask, turning to Betty. "Who's the lucky fella?"

"Al's taking me to the diner over in River Hollow for breakfast." Betty's words are casual, but her face flushes, and she's suddenly absorbed in the task of washing her hands.

Liv and I exchange a look. Betty's usually very open about her dates. I've never seen her this flustered talking about a man before.

"Speaking of gentleman callers." Betty turns off the faucet and dries her hands on a dishrag. "I couldn't help but notice a certain truck pulling out of the driveway late last night." She waggles her eyebrows at me.

My chest burns redder than Ty's pickup. I hadn't broached the topic of Ty with Betty and Liv yet. I didn't know how to after spending the past week insisting that the two of us were never going to get back together.

"What?" Liv's to-go cup falls from her hand, plonking onto the tabletop. It tips over, spilling her vanilla latte everywhere. She doesn't make a move to clean it up. "You hooked up with Ty?" Her eyes are wide, and she clasps her palms to her heart like she's about to do some second-hand swooning. "Does this mean you're back together?"

"I, um..." I stammer, glancing over at Betty. She gives me a wicked grin, and I sigh. "Okay, yes. I did, and maybe?" I grab the roll of paper towels off the counter again and start mopping up Liv's coffee, trying to hide the love-sick smile sneaking across my face.

Liv squeals, leaping out of her chair and smashing me in a hug. The towel falls from my hand with a wet whump. "I knew it. You two are totally soulmates. How did it happen? I demand details."

"I'll tell you what happened," Betty says. "Ty showed up at her door and was like..." She reaches into a drawer and pulls out a spatula, raising it to her lips like a microphone. "Baby, give me one more chaaaaaance." Betty launches into a surprisingly decent song and dance routine, and Liv jumps in with backup vocals.

I cover my burning face with my hands but can't help laughing. "Keep it up, and I'm signing the two of you up for karaoke tonight."

Naturally, they ignore me, continuing to belt out lyrics. I'm simultaneously mortified and amused, which is a very familiar feeling. They lovingly harassed me the entire time Ty and I were together. My phone vibrates in my pocket, and I glance at the screen. It's a FaceTime call from my dad.

I slash a hand in front of my throat, motioning for Betty and Liv to cease and desist. "It's my dad." I hold up my cell to show them the incoming call.

I do not need them singing songs about me getting back with my ex while I'm talking to my father. Discussing my love life with him would be about as pleasant as a root canal. To say he wasn't Ty's biggest fan after he got me arrested and expelled would be an understatement.

Liv and Betty quit singing but continue shooting me roguish glances. I shake my head at them and swipe to answer the call.

"Hey, kiddo!" Dad grins out at me.

"Hi, Dad."

"What are you up to?"

"Oh, you know. Just doing crafts with Betty and Liv." I try to sound offhand and casual like nothing earth-shattering recently happened.

Dad's eyebrows lift in surprise. "You three are doing crafts?"

Sometimes I forget how well he knows us Kelley girls. I might have turned myself into a first-rate baker, but that took a lot of work. Domesticity isn't typically our strong suit.

"We sure are," Betty chimes in from over my shoulder. "See." She waves her mangled scrunchie in front of the camera.

"Wow." Dad nods, and I can tell he's holding back a laugh. "That's really something."

"It's something, alright," I mutter, and Betty bumps me with her hip.

"So, listen, hun." My dad says. "Betty told me about all the effort you've put into the festival this week. Carrie and I thought we'd check out the movie night and see all your hard work in action."

"You and Carrie are coming to Rosedale?" Excitement over seeing my dad wars with the dread of having to make small talk with Carrie. I don't know what to say to her after our last encounter.

"Yeah. It's been a couple of months since I've been down there, and I miss you."

"I miss you too,"

"Carrie's excited to see you again. She feels terrible about what happened and wants to make it up to you." The glint in Dad's eyes is pleading. It clearly means a lot to him that I get along with Carrie. He works so hard to help me, and I know how much he loves me. There isn't much I wouldn't do for him. If Carrie's important to him, then I need to give her another chance.

I sigh inwardly and nod, forcing a smile onto my face. "That sounds perfect."

The grin that lights up my dad's face makes any impending awkwardness with Carrie worth it. "Great. We'll see you tomorrow, then."

"See you tomorrow." I blow a kiss at the phone, and Dad disconnects the call.

"That was the right thing to do," Betty says from where she's leaning against the kitchen counter.

"Yeah, well." I shrug. I'm about to set my cell on the table when it buzzes in my hand. I glance down at the screen and freeze as I stare at the text from Janet. The air leaves my lungs in a whoosh. It's as though my insides have evaporated, leaving me hollow and dazed.

"What's wrong?" Liv takes in my expression, and her forehead furrows with concern.

My mouth is moving, but no words are coming out because no. There's no way this is right. I read the message again.

Janet: Just wanted to make sure you got your grant application submitted yesterday. Let me know how it went. Remember, I believe in you!

"No. No. No. No. No." I whisper as I text Janet back. This can't be happening.

Me: Yesterday? You said it was due next Wednesday.

My heart's in my throat as I watch the three dots dance on the screen. "Type faster, Janet," I growl. I can feel Betty and Liv watching me, but I can't think beyond those dots. If their flickering doesn't end with Janet saying she's just kidding, I don't know what I'm going to do. My phone finally buzzes with her response. My stomach plummets so far; it must have relocated somewhere near my ankle.

Janet: Oh, no! Quinn, I said that last Friday. I highlighted the due date in the email I sent you.

It's not possible. I open my email app and reread her message. Sure enough, yesterday's date glows up at me in bright yellow. How did I not notice that? I'm meticulous in everything I do. This was the most important deadline of my life. It's unfathomable that I could have overlooked it. But I did. I let myself get swept up in the festival and in Ty. I blew the best shot I had to make my counseling business a reality.

Another text from Janet comes through.

Janet: I'm so sorry! I should've followed up with you earlier. You're always so on top of things. I didn't think you needed me to.

I can feel my dreams shattering into pieces around me. My fingers tap out a response on their own. My mind is nothing but white noise.

Me: It's not your fault, Janet. Thanks for trying.

I hit send and let my phone drop to the table with a clatter. When I glance up, Betty and Liv are watching me, matching expressions of worry on their faces.

"Quinn," Betty says carefully, like I'm an animal she doesn't want to spook. "What happened, sweetie?"

I'm too hollowed out to cry as I say, "I missed the deadline for the grant."

They don't say anything; just wrap me in a hug as all my hope for the future drains out of me.

Chapter 25

My shoes squeak against the linoleum as I run out the cafeteria doors to the truck, idling at the curb. I grab as many folding chairs out of the back as I can carry. They clang together as I hustle back inside to add them to the rows we've already set up. The familiar scent of floor wax and fried food makes me want to gag.

We were supposed to have the karaoke night in the high school gymnasium, but someone in the administration forgot the event was tonight and had the floor re-finished this morning, making it impossible to walk on. We relocated to the cafeteria. But since the chairs in here are attached to the tables, I had to contact a party planning company about delivering an emergency stash of folding chairs. They just barely got here, and people will begin arriving for the festival in about—I glance down at my watch—ten minutes. Crap.

"Test. Test. Test." Chance taps the microphone. The speakers he placed around the room give a screech of feedback. I wince, clapping my hands over my ears. He's been unsuccessfully trying to get them to work for the last half an hour, which is consistent with how the rest of my day's gone so far.

Al's crew accidentally cut the power to the freezers at the cooking school without realizing it. The gourmet parfait popsicles Giselle was going to pass out tonight melted into a giant gooey mess, leaving us with no refreshments to serve. I put up a post on the town's Facebook page, asking everyone to bring their own treats, which received a slew of unhappy comments that I'm doing my best not to pay attention to.

To top it all off, I've had to handle everything myself since Ty is MIA. I've been calling and texting all day and have gotten no reply. At first, I was confused and hurt that he wouldn't answer after everything he said last night. But after a couple hours of total radio silence, I started getting irritated.

I'm already devastated over missing the deadline for the grant, especially since Liv put together such a fantastic video submission. My dad and I still haven't found any solutions to my prescription situation. The stress of trying to figure out how I'm going to navigate my impending financial crisis is overwhelming and terrifying. I really didn't need to deal with all of this alone today, especially when my supposedly on-again boyfriend should have been here, helping me.

I whirl on my heel to pick up another load of chairs and notice Giselle on the other side of the cafeteria. She's tying bunches of balloons to the end of each row. It's no easy feat to make a high school cafeteria look festive, but she certainly gets an A for effort. I give her a grateful wave as I jog past.

I'm out of breath, chest heaving, by the time I reach the cargo hold. Relief floods through me when I see there are only four chairs left.

"Thank God." I hoist them out of the truck, fully intending to bail the second this show is up and running. I'm going to go home, make myself some AIP cookie dough, and try to come up with a strategy to salvage my life plan.

"Can I help with those?" A voice says from behind me.

I freeze, squeezing my eyes shut. Last night, that voice was making promises to me about our future together. Promises that were clearly forgotten by this morning.

I turn to face Ty. His smile is heart-achingly genuine, like he's actually happy to see me when he hasn't replied to any of my text messages. My traitorous stomach flitters at the sight of him, which only makes me madder. How dare he show up here, acting like everything's fine after he spent the entire day pretending I don't exist?

"I've got them," I snap, brushing past him.

"Quinn, wait." Ty's fingers wrap around my shoulder.

"Don't touch me." I turn around, jerking out of his grasp.

Surprise and hurt flash across Ty's features, and his hand falls limply to his side. "Why are you mad?"

The legs of the chairs jangle together as I drop them on the ground. I blink at Ty. "Why am I mad? Are you serious?"

Ty's forehead crumples in confusion. "Okay, what happened? When I left last night, you were...happy."

Happy doesn't begin to describe what I was last night. When Ty kissed me goodbye, I was lost in a haze of bliss. I was in love. It's mind-boggling how quickly things can change.

"Well, that was before I spent hours calling and texting the guy who's supposed to be my boyfriend again, and he didn't even bother to respond." I grab the chairs and stomp past Ty into the cafeteria.

"Jeeze, Quinn." Ty catches up to me. His eyes dart around the room, which is already filling with people. His face flushes as though I'm embarrassing him. "I'm sorry I couldn't answer the phone, but I was busy today."

I swallow. Part of me was holding out hope that maybe he'd lost his cell or something, but he really was just choosing to ignore me. Awesome.

"Busy with what, Ty?" I ask.

His mouth opens like he's finally going to tell me what's going on with him. But then he snaps it shut and shakes his head. "I can't talk about it yet. I told you, I need you to be patient."

"Yeah, well, I needed you today." My anger gives way to bone-deep disappointment because I did need him. Not only to help with the festival chaos but to be there for me when I was stressed and scared and felt like my future was starting to slip out of my control again.

Last night, I was ready to give my whole heart back to Ty. But what's he expecting me to do? Sit around, waiting for him while I have no idea where he is or what he's doing? And meanwhile, I can't even expect him to return a freaking phone call? No. I stride toward the back row, flipping open the chairs and sliding them into place.

Someone dims the fluorescent lights, and I glance over to where the karaoke DJ's setting up his equipment. People are filing into the rows, snatching up the best seats. Some of them have downloaded the karaoke company's app and are perusing the catalog of available songs. I weave between the aisles to the DJ's table to make sure everything's good to go.

"Quinn, come on. Talk to me," Ty says from behind my shoulder.

This guy seriously has quite the pair. He shows up here, demanding I speak to him after he screened my calls. I spin to face him. "I tried to talk to you. All day, in fact. You were too busy, so I'm done."

Ty opens his mouth to say something, but I turn my back on him.

"Hi. Are we good to go here?" I ask the DJ.

"I'm all set. Just waiting on your friend to finish with the mic." He jerks a thumb toward Chance, who's still playing with the microphone. Chance has been working part-time for Rock the Mic since we were in high school. He wants to be a big-time DJ one day. Unfortunately, I've witnessed his complete lack of rhythm on multiple occasions and have doubts about the viability of that career path for him.

I sigh and march toward Chance. This day cannot be over soon enough.

"What do you mean you're done?" Ty demands, hot on my heels.

I don't turn around. "I can't deal with this right now, Ty. One of us has to make sure this event actually happens."

The room buzzes with conversation. Gary's hovering near the front row, humming off-pitch octaves to warm up his vocal cords.

"Is that thing going to be ready anytime soon?" I bark at Chance.

Chance's brows lift in surprise at the sharp edge in my tone. "Yeah. I think we're good." He flips a switch on the microphone and taps it once. A thump echoes through the speakers, but thankfully there's no feedback this time. I wave a hand to get the DJ's attention and give him a thumbs-up.

He leans toward the mic stand on his table and says, "Helloooooo, Rosedale! Who's ready to sing?" Everyone whoops and cheers, and I sag with relief and exhaustion.

"I am!" Gary cries, bolting to the front of the room and taking his place behind the microphone. Liv lets out a loud catcall from the audience.

I walk to the side of the room and lean against the wall. My feet are throbbing from running around. I'm just going to watch Gary and make sure everything's going smoothly. Then I'm hibernating with my cookie dough until I have to leave my cave for the movie night tomorrow.

From my peripheral vision, I see Ty come to stand next to me. He folds his arms over his chest. "Are you really just going to ignore me now?" His voice is equal parts irritation and heartache.

Well, he's not the only one hurting. How did he think I'd react after his disappearing routine?

"That depends. Are you going to tell me why you didn't call me back?" I don't look at Ty. Just stare blankly at Gary as the opening notes of 'I Don't Want to Miss a Thing' resonate through the cafeteria. Gary's eyes are fixed on the monitor propped on a folding chair next to the mic.

"I told you I can't," Ty growls as though I'm the one who's out of line here.

"Well, I can't—"

Gary's voice rings through the air, cutting me off. But...it isn't his voice. Not unless he's been transfigured into Alvin from Alvin and the Chipmunks. What the heck?

Gary breaks off, staring at the microphone in confusion. He turns it off and on again, then shrugs. He skims the words on the monitor, trying to find his place before taking a big breath and attempting to belt out the chorus. But again, his voice comes squeaking through the sound system like a cartoon rodent.

Snickers trickle through the crowd, and that's when I notice them. Chance and Kelvin, standing on the other side of the room, bent over laughing. I glance from them to the microphone Chance was fiddling with all afternoon and put the pieces together. They've swapped out the regular mic with a trick one. How did I not see this coming? Everything makes so much sense now.

I laugh, but it's humorless and ugly. "So, that's what you were up to today?" I turn to Ty. "Buying some stupid prank microphone?"

"What are you talking about? I didn't have anything to do with that." Ty gestures toward Gary, whose face is turning beet red. Gary's so flustered his glasses are fogging up. He swipes a finger inside the lenses to clean them.

I know exactly how it feels to be the person on the receiving end of those idiots' pranks. Gary might be a bit ridiculous, but he cares about this town and the festival. He's been practicing all week. He doesn't deserve to be turned into a laughingstock.

"I hope you're proud of yourself," I mutter as the DJ cuts the music and hurries over to swap his real mic with Gary's fake one.

"Are you just determined to sabotage what we have together? I. Didn't. Do. This." Ty enunciates each word as though I don't believe him because I'm slow and not because I've been burned too many times before.

"I'm sabotaging us? You're the one who's been ignoring me and won't even tell me why!"

"Because my mom had cancer, okay!" Ty yells. He throws his hands up in frustration.

He might as well have lobbed a grenade. The repercussion steals the air from my lungs, leaving me stunned and utterly gutted.

"What?" My voice is less than a whisper. The music starts again, but it's hardly a blip on my radar. It sounds like it's coming from somewhere far, far away, like someone filled my ears with cotton.

Ty rakes his hands through his hair. "She had thyroid cancer. She had to have it removed, and she's been in isolation at a hospital in the city while she did radiation. She was released today, and we got to go bring her home. So I'm sorry that I wasn't available to take your calls or help with karaoke night. But I've been a little preoccupied."

My body processes his words before my mind does. Tears slip down my cheeks without warning. I don't know if I'm sad, angry, or just feel incredibly guilty. "Why didn't you tell me?"

"She didn't want anyone to know." Ty blinks, staring at the beat-up linoleum like he's on the verge of crying too. He drags his eyes up to mine, and the devastation simmering there shatters me. "You're never going to believe in me, are you?" he says. "No matter what I do, you'll never be able to leave the past behind us."

There are so many things I should be saying to him right now. That I do believe in him. That I believe in us. That I overreacted because I'm so stressed out about my future and finances that it's taking everything I have just to keep breathing. But I'm too shattered by the news about his mom to make my mouth form words.

Ty must mistake my silence for agreement. He bites his trembling lips together and nods once. "Bye, Quinn."

I reach out a hand to try and stop him, to offer any comfort I can, but I'm too late. He's already walking away from me.

Chapter 26

'm out the cafeteria door and across the parking lot before I realize what I'm doing. A chill has settled deep in my bones, and I shiver despite the warm night air. I'm so numb; it's like I'm sleepwalking. I can't think over the buzzing in my ears. I'm dimly aware that there are things I need to do. I have to get myself home. I have to call Ty. But I can't focus on the present moment long enough to guide my feet in any logical direction. The present hurts too much.

The last time I felt like this was when I found out about my mom's car accident. It's like it's happening all over again. Like I'm about to have another hole ripped through my life, leaving me empty and devastated.

Lucia's barely middle-aged. She's always been so healthy and full of life. I want to believe she'll beat this, that she'll be fine. But once you've experienced unexpected and soul-wrenching loss, it's hard to trust that it won't happen again.

I didn't even ask Ty how Lucia was doing or if her treatments worked. He probably thinks I'm the world's biggest jerk. I am the world's biggest jerk. He was with his mother, who's been fighting cancer, and I was pissed at him for not returning my phone calls about karaoke night? What is wrong with me?

"Quinn!" I'm halfway down Liger Lane when I realize someone's been shouting my name.

"Quinn, wait!" I turn to see Liv sprinting toward me. I stop walking, watching as she hurries down the road.

My feet are aching, and my arms are already stiff from carrying all those chairs. But I observe the pain distantly, like it's happening to someone else. If I let myself really feel those small hurts, it'll open the door for all the much bigger ones to come barreling through. I'm not sure I can survive it.

Liv catches up to me. She bends forward, clutching her knees. "Where are you going?" she asks between pants.

"Home." My voice is so lifeless and devoid of emotion I hardly recognize it.

"Home is that way." Liv jerks her thumb in the opposite direction. The worried lines etched across her forehead deepen. "Quinn, you're freaking me out. What happened?"

"Lucia has cancer." The words taste wrong on my tongue, bitter and false. I can't believe they're real.

"No," Liv gasps. Her hands fly to her mouth. "Is she alright? What did Ty tell you?"

The only thing I can think to say is, "I don't know."

I turn and start walking again because moving is better than standing still. It gives me something to focus on other than the wrecked expression on Ty's face when he told me about his mother's illness. I concentrate on each step, the way the cobblestones press unevenly against the soles of my shoes.

"Quinn, stop!" Liv grabs my wrist. "Tell me what happened."

"I can't!" My words explode from deep inside me, echoing off the nearby houses. I yank my arm out of Liv's grasp. Her eyes go wide in surprise and alarm.

A small voice in my mind is screaming at me not to take this out on Liv. She doesn't deserve it, and I know that. But she's also trying to force me to talk about things I'm not ready to deal with yet. And now that I've started yelling, I can't stop. The dam holding back my flood of emotions has broken.

"I can't tell you what's going on because I didn't even ask! I'm horrible. I deserve all the awful things that keep happening to me. I deserve to be sick. To not be able to afford anything. To have Ty leave me again. Because I'm terrible. I didn't ask. I mean, seriously, what kind of person wouldn't ask?"

It isn't until I feel something wet against my cheek that I realize I'm crying again. My breath's coming in gasps, making my vision go sparkly. I wobble on my feet, grasping at the empty air for balance.

"Quinn, breathe." Liv's face pales, and she reaches out a hand to steady me, but my legs give way before she can. I collapse onto the street, butt-bones smacking into the hard ground as everything I hadn't let myself feel slams into me at once. I wrap my arms around my knees, and sobs wrack my body. I'm drowning in worry, and fear, and heartbreak. I don't know how to find my way to the surface.

Liv kneels in front of me. "Listen to me," she says softly. I look up. Her face is nothing but a blur through my stream of tears. "I'm not sure what happened back there, but you're a wonderful person. The best I know. If you didn't say the right thing, it's because you're in shock. Ty will forgive you."

I cling to her words like a life raft in a sea of hopelessness. I want to believe them, despite how unlikely it seems that they could be true.

"I messed up. I messed everything up," I say between sobs.

"Okay, I need you to tell me what you mean by that, but first, we've got to get you out of the road."

I nod, sending tears scattering across the cobblestones. I'm so grateful the entire town is currently in the school cafeteria, so nobody else is here to see me crumble. Liv's fingers close around my upper arms, and she helps me to the curb. I slump onto the concrete.

"Alright, lay it on me, sister." Liv sits down next to me and rubs circles across my back.

I blow out a shuddering breath and scrub at my tear-soaked cheeks. "He wasn't answering my calls," I blurt because I have no idea where else to begin explaining how badly I screwed everything up.

"Ty?"

"Yes. Everything was going wr-wrong with the stupid karaoke night, and I kept calling him and texting him. And he wouldn't respond, and I didn't know w-why," I stammer. "I got mad, and I y-yelled at him." I turn to look at Liv because I need to see the look on her face when I say this. Need to know if she thinks I'm as terrible as I feel.

"His mom's been getting treatments for thyroid cancer. He had to pick her up from the hospital today. He said he was busy, and I just couldn't accept that as an answer." A fresh surge of tears spills down my face. "But I didn't know, Liv. He didn't tell me."

"Oh, Quinn." Liv's eyebrows furrow, but in sympathy, not judgment. She pulls me into a tight hug. The street light flickers on above us, casting the road in an orange glow. "That's not your fault. Ty should've told you about his mom."

"I'm going to lose him again." My voice is tiny, barely audible over the sound of crickets chirping in the fields behind us.

Liv shakes her head. "You won't lose him. But you have to talk to him this time. You need to tell him why you were so upset today."

"What if he won't speak to me?"

"He will."

At the doubtful expression on my face, Liv takes hold of my shoulders and gives me a playful little shake, trying to lighten the moment. "He will."

I attempt a smile, but my lips tremble. I bite them together to keep from crying again. "I'm losing control of everything. I missed the deadline for the grant. My insurance isn't going to help pay for my medication anymore. I'm terrified I won't be able to afford it, and I'll get sick again. And Ty—" I swallow the lump in my throat. "Ty's going to break up with me." I bury my face in my knees.

"Shhh." Liv strokes a calming hand through my hair. "None of those things are going to happen."

"You don't know that."

"I don't," Liv admits. "But I do know you're doing your absolute best. And if you don't start trusting that that's enough and stop trying to control the outcome of every situation, you'll give yourself a nervous breakdown."

I turn my head so my cheek's resting against my knees as I look over at her. "I don't think I know how to do that."

"You don't say. You're usually so chill." Liv shoots me a grin and bumps my shoulder with hers. A watery laugh escapes my lips. "I know it doesn't feel like it right now," she says, "but everything's going to work out. I promise." Her words are so full of certainty I almost believe them.

"How?" I ask.

"I'm not sure." She shrugs, staring up at the glittering stars. "But I'm here for you, and so is Mom. We'll figure it out together."

Life's knocked me down so many times. But with Liv, Betty, and Dad's help, I've always managed to pick up the pieces. As impossible as it seems to stop worrying and believe everything will be fine Liv's right. I can't keep going like this. I need to trust in my people and in myself. We all deserve at least that much.

"Thank you." I lean my head on Liv's shoulder, and she sits with me until the ache in my chest eases enough that I can take a full breath.

Chapter 27

I set the box of triple-chocolate-chunk cookies on the passenger seat of Betty's Prius before hurrying around to the driver's side and climbing in. I have a special delivery to make this morning, and Betty was nice enough to let me borrow her car. I rest my hand on the box as I pull onto Main Street. I'd really like to deliver these cookies in one piece this time.

The scent of sugar and chocolate fills the car, making my mouth water. Driving past the park, I notice that the rental company is already setting up the outdoor movie screen and projector. Thank goodness. It would be such a relief if everything went smoothly tonight. To say I could use a break after yesterday's mayhem is an understatement.

I'm doing my best not to dwell on how badly I blew my shot at the Happy Spoons Grant, but it's hard. My natural inclination is to fixate on an issue—real or imagined—until I'm satisfied that I can control the outcome. Trusting that everything will work out is hard for me, especially since I don't have a plan for how I'll be able to pay for my medications. Forget about launching my business.

But I'm not alone in this. I've got Liv and Betty, and I've got my dad too. Between the four of us, I'm sure we'll be able to figure out a solution. Or at least that's what I keep telling myself. It will take a lot of practice for me to stop living in a constant state of panic over the future. I keep catching myself starting to slip back into worry mode. But as Janet would say, you don't have to be great to start, but you do have to start to be great. And this is the beginning of an all-new Quinn, one who's less controlling and hopefully much less stressed out.

I turn onto the aptly-named Poplar Street. It's lined on either side with giant trees that cast long shadows across the road in the early-morning light. The air has that warm, fuzzy quality it only gets on clear summer mornings. It's peaceful and lulls me into a sleepy haze, making me yawn.

I didn't get much sleep. Trying to let go of my anxiety over my own future is hard enough. Keeping myself from worrying about Lucia's health is impossible when I have almost no information about what's happening. I was too emotionally wrung out to call Ty last night and ask him for more details. Not that he would've answered anyway. I understand why he didn't tell me what was going on. But I still wish he'd felt like he could confide in me. If anyone understands what he's going through, it's me.

I haven't exactly been making it easy for him to talk to me lately, though. I've been too concerned about whether or not he was going to break my heart again. I have a tendency to believe the worst in people. It feels safer to expect everyone to let you down, like it'll hurt less if you see it coming. But it never works out that way. It still stings just as much when someone disappoints you, and I know I disappointed Ty. I'm the one who owes him an apology this time, and I need to do it in person.

I park the car in front of the Rossi's farm-style house. Everything about it says 'home' from the yellow clapboard siding and cherry-red door to the picket fence. Being inside is like having someone wrap you in a hug. Love permeates every room.

Grabbing the cookies, I unlatch the gate and walk up to the door. My heart's humming, and I pause to gather my courage before knocking. I'm not sure what kind of reception I'll get showing up like this.

I take a breath and rap my knuckles against the door. There aren't any sounds coming from inside the house, and I fight to stop my mind from spiraling into what-ifs. What if Ty told his family I yelled at him, and none of them want to speak to me? What if something went wrong, and they had to rush Lucia back to the hospital? But after a few seconds, I hear the steady tread of feet against tile, and the door swings open.

"Quinn, what a wonderful surprise." Gianna holds out an arm, giving me a big side-hug and being careful not to smash the box I'm holding. I blink my eyes to keep them from welling up. I really needed that hug today. I didn't even know how much. Gianna pulls back but keeps her hands on my shoulders. "I'm afraid you missed Ty, hun. He already left for work."

"I'm actually not here for Ty," I say. I made sure his truck was safely parked outside the cooking school before driving over here. I need to apologize to him, but I have a couple other things to take care of first. "I was hoping to see Lucia. If she's feeling up to it, that is."

A somber smile stretches across Gianna's face, and her eyes spark with understanding. "Ty finally told you."

I bite my lip and nod. Ty must not have told his family about our conversation yesterday, which is a relief. I'd be humiliated if they all knew what a monster I was being. But I also don't want them to be mad at Ty for telling me about Lucia's situation.

"He did," I admit. "But he didn't want to. I um...I kind of forced it out of him."

Gianna squeezes my arms. "I'm glad. He needs someone to talk to right now. This has been hard on him."

My eyes drop to the ground, and I swallow. I know how much Ty loves his mother. I'm sure he's needed a friend recently, and I haven't been that for him. I might have plenty of reasons for that, but I still regret it. If I could rewind to a week ago when Ty first got back to town, I'd do everything differently. I just hope he'll give me another chance.

Gianna inhales and eyes the box I'm holding. "Are those Nelson's triple-chocolate-chunk cookies?"

A small smile tugs at my lips, and I shrug. "Of course. Only the best for Lucia."

"Well, you better get in here then." She steps inside and gestures for me to follow her. "Everyone else left for the day, but Mama's in the living room, and she's going to be very happy to see you."

Chapter 28

Walking into the foyer is like stepping back in time. The buttercream color on the walls is exactly as I remember it, and the grooves of the hardwood floor are as familiar as the lines on the palm of my hand. But it's the small changes that make my heart twinge. New photographs have been hung. A turquoise-patterned rug I've never seen decorates the hallway. I spent so much time here when I was with Ty; it felt like home. Seeing the little updates they've made to the house makes me realize how much I've missed.

It takes all my concentration to keep my chin from wobbling. I'm not about to dump my emotional baggage on Lucia. She has more than enough to deal with already.

"Mama, look who's here to see you. She brought your favorite cookies, too," Gianna says as I trail her into the living room.

Lucia's sitting on the couch, legs curled underneath her. She's staring at the television screen, blanket draped over her shoulders. Her shiny dark hair is shorter than the last time I saw her. It's cut in a bob, and she's pushed the strands back behind her ears. She glances over at me, and her umber-colored eyes light up with a smile.

"Quinn! Get your darling butt in here and give this old lady a hug." Lucia pushes herself off the sofa and holds out her arms. A bandage covers her throat, and she looks a little tired. But otherwise, she's the same Lucia I've always known, charismatic and full of life.

Gianna takes the cookies from me and sets them on the coffee table before sitting in the plush leather armchair next to the fireplace.

"Lucia, how are you?" I'm careful as I put my arms around her, not wanting to hurt her.

"I'm just fine." Lucia pulls back and wags a finger at me. "Now, none of this nonsense. I'm not made of glass. I want a real hug." She squeezes me tight, and I laugh, hugging her back. "That's more like it," she says.

She sits back on the sofa and pats the cushion next to her. "Come, tell me what's new with you, so I'll stop watching this rubbish." She motions toward the television where Married at First Sight is playing. "I got hooked on it while I was in the hospital, and now I'm too invested to quit."

"Nothing new here," I say. "I'm still working on my nutrition certification and teaching classes for Giselle." My entire world has imploded in the past week, but I didn't come here to talk about myself and my problems.

Lucia's always been able to see right through me. She narrows her eyes like she doesn't believe me, but she lets it slide. "Well, it sounds like you're staying as busy as ever. And you look beautiful. So healthy."

"Thank you." I smile feebly. It feels wrong that I should get to be healthy when she hasn't been. I'm used to being the person struggling with illnesses. Being on the other side is unfamiliar territory. "I'm so sorry I didn't reach out sooner," I say. "I had no idea you were sick."

Lucia sighs and shakes her head. "That son of mine. I told him I didn't want everyone to know, but I assumed he knew you were an exception. You're practically part of the family." She looks to Gianna for confirmation.

Gianna bobs her head. "That's what I kept telling him."

Hearing them say that heals a tiny piece of my heart. No matter what happens with Ty, I'll always adore his family. I hate that Lucia's been going through something this serious, and I didn't even know about it.

"I didn't want the whole town finding out I was sick and treating me like some kind of invalid." Lucia points at me. "I know you can relate to that."

I huff out a laugh. "Boy, can I ever." If Jenny Jenkins offers me her sweater again at the park tonight, my head may actually implode. The last thing I ever want to do is make Lucia feel like I see her as an illness and not the strong, capable woman she is. But I care about her so much it's killing me not to know the details about her prognosis.

"If you don't want to talk about health stuff, I completely understand," I say. "But can I ask how your treatments are going? Ty didn't tell me much."

"You can ask anything you want. You brought me chocolate-chunk cookies." Lucia nods at the box and pats my hand. "I'm going to be fine. It's always scary when a doctor says, 'cancer.' Such an ugly, awful word." Lucia shudders.

I can't imagine how terrifying it would be to get that news. Finding out about my own chronic illness was stressful enough.

"But this type of cancer is very treatable," Lucia continues. "They did a full thyroid removal." She touches her fingertips to the bandage on her neck. "We also did radiation just to be safe, and I'll have to go in regularly for check-ups to make sure it doesn't come back." Lucia picks up a glass of water from the coffee table and takes a sip. "We're still figuring out the right doses for my hormone replacements. But I'm going to heal up, and I'll be better than ever. Mark my words."

"I'm so glad to hear that." I squeeze Lucia's hand. Her optimism is contagious. I wish I could bottle it. "Are they helping you with your diet?" I ask. "You know, food can really make a big difference when you're experiencing changes in body chemistry."

"Why do I need doctors to help me with my diet when I have you? Consider me your first client."

This woman is determined to make me cry by the time I leave the house. My eyes burn, and I swallow down the emotion trying to bubble up. "I'd be honored. I'm not finished with my certification yet, but I can work with my advisor to put together a meal plan for you. Then you can run it all past your doctors before we get started."

"That sounds wonderful, but," Lucia holds up a finger, "you better not try to make me give up my cannolis."

I laugh. "I wouldn't dare."

"Good girl. Speaking of cannolis, I hear my Ty did really well at the bake sale this year." There's no mistaking the glint of pride in Lucia's eyes.

My jaw drops. "Wait. Are you saying Ty made those?" He didn't say a word about baking the cannolis himself. I'm positive I heard people telling him to give their compliments to Lucia, and he didn't correct them. It makes sense that he wouldn't want to explain why he had to be the one to bake them, though.

"He made them all himself," Gianna grins. "Mama taught him everything she knows."

"Well, I couldn't send him off to college without knowing how to make a decent cannoli. What kind of mother would I be?" Lucia waves her hands as she speaks. She can't help but put her whole self into every word she says. It's one of the many things I've always loved about her. "And you better believe he's taking that recipe straight back to California come spring semester. I can't have him risking his education just so he can go to follow-up appointments with me. I would've refused to let him stay here during fall semester if he'd bothered to ask. Stubborn boy." She shakes her head in fond exasperation.

A pang of tenderness pulses through me. That sounds like Ty, alright.

"Of all people, I can't believe he didn't tell you he made those cannolis, though." Lucia shoots me a meaningful look. "I thought that he'd be trying to impress you."

"Oh, um. We aren't really— " My words trail off, and I dig my teeth into my lip. I can feel my chest and neck going splotchy as an awkward silence falls over the room. I have no idea how to finish that sentence.

Understanding washes over Lucia's features, and she exchanges a glance with Gianna. "My son is a good boy," she says. "But sometimes, he pays too much attention to what's happening up here."

She taps her temple. "And not enough attention to what's happening in here." She rests a hand over her heart. "All the most important things that happen in life happen in here." She pats her chest again and raises her eyebrows at me, making it clear she isn't just talking about Ty.

Her words echo what Betty and Liv have been saying—that I need to stop overthinking everything and start trusting in myself and my heart. If these smart, incredible women are all saying the same thing, they can't be wrong. I might struggle to believe everything will work out for me, but I do believe in them. And I know what my heart's been telling me ever since Ty came back to town. It's time I started listening to it, even if it means taking the risk of having it broken all over again. Lucia's watching me closely, waiting for my response.

I force myself to take a breath and nod. "I hear you."

"Do you?" Lucia squints her eyes, scrutinizing me like she isn't convinced.

I can't blame her. I don't have the greatest track record of following my heart. And when I don't, her son usually ends up getting hurt in the process. Ty certainly isn't blameless when it comes to the current state of our relationship, but that doesn't mean I can't be the one to try and fix it. I need to tell Ty how I feel, even if it's hard. Even if it's painful. Because the possibility that I might get to be with him again makes the risk worth it.

"I do." A grin creeps across my face, despite the nerves attempting to turn my stomach inside out. "In fact, I should probably get going. I have a phone call to make if I'm going to win that boy of yours back."

"Thatta girl." Lucia beams, and Gianna claps her hands and says, "Finally."

I stand and hug each of them again. "Will I see you at the movie night?"

"We wouldn't miss it." Lucia winks at me. "Oh, and Quinn?"

"Yeah?"

"Good luck." She plants a kiss on my cheek.

"Thanks." I place a hand on my jittery stomach. "I'm gonna need it."

Lucia gives me a knowing look and pats my arm. "These things have a way of working out. You wait and see."

The old Quinn was never great at waiting, but the new Quinn's ready to put her heart on her sleeve and see where it leads her. I just hope Lucia's right.

Chapter 29

My heart's beating so fast, it literally hurts. I press a palm to my chest and force myself to take a steady breath as I scan the park. Everything appears in order. The lights decorating the trees and gazebo glow against the periwinkle sky. People have been stopping by all day to claim their spots. Blankets in every color of the rainbow are spread over the lawn. The giant screen and projector are ready to go, and Giselle's already set up the refreshment table with a variety of gourmet popcorn balls.

There's nothing left for me to do but announce the movie and thank everyone for their participation in the festival this week. Usually, speaking in front of everybody would turn me into a hot, shaky mess. But that's the least of my worries tonight.

I'm going to apologize to Ty and ask him to give us another chance. Because the only thing scarier than baring my heart to him would be not to. If he rejects me, at least I'll know I tried. I can't live with the idea of letting us fall apart again without telling him how I feel. I just hope he shows up.

I thought he might be here early to help get everything ready, but I haven't seen him. Each minute that passes makes the knot in my stomach double in size. I'm terrified he's not going to come. That he's going to disappear on me again.

Lucia said these things have a way of working out, and I don't think she'd encourage me to pursue her son if she thought it was a lost cause. But there's no guarantee things will go how I want them to. I'm doing my best to let go of the need to try and control the outcome, but the anticipation is so heavy it might actually crush me.

"Hey there, hot stuff. What can we help with?" I turn to see Liv and Betty cutting across the lawn toward me. Betty's got her hair pulled up in a messy ponytail with her neon-green scrunchie.

I grin. Having them here eases some of the panic I've been fighting to keep at bay. "I think we're ready." I wave a hand, gesturing around the park. It looks like a set out of a Hallmark movie.

"Hmmm." Betty scans the lawn and bunches her lips to the side. "How mad do you think the owner of that hot-pink Minky would be if we swapped places with them?"

I glance over at the fuzzy, pink blanket in the middle of the front row. "Well, considering the owner is Gary and you don't even have a spot yet..." I tilt my head toward the red-and-white-checkered throw in her arms. "I'd guess pretty mad."

"Rats. I knew we should've cut French Toast Friday short." She frowns and goes to lay their blanket out on a patch of grass beneath a giant maple tree. I can't help noticing Al and a few of his crew members standing nearby, chatting. Betty gives him a wave and fiddles nervously with her ponytail.

"What do you think of that?" I ask Liv.

Liv follows my gaze and shrugs. "She's in the butterfly stage. We'll see if she's still all googly-eyed next week." She lowers her voice and glances around. "Is Ty here?"

"Not yet." I try to keep my smile in place despite the fresh cracks tracing themselves across my heart.

Liv squeezes my arm. "He'll be here."

I nod, but I can't meet her eyes. I'm afraid if I see any sympathy there, I'll dissolve into a puddle of uncertainty.

"You better have brought the tissues," Betty says to Liv as she walks back to us. "We're officially in nose-bleed territory."

Liv rolls her eyes. "The screen's, like, twenty-five feet away, you drama queen."

"It's the principle." Betty narrows her eyes at her, but then her gaze lands on something over my shoulder, and she brightens. "Oh, hey! Look who's here."

My mind immediately goes to Ty, and my stomach tries to catapult itself into my throat. I whirl around. It isn't Ty, but it's almost as good.

"Dad!" I squeal and run across the street to where he parked his Ford Fusion.

"Oof," he grunts, laughing as I launch myself into his arms. "Hi, kiddo."

He's got at least six inches on me, so I have to crane my neck to look up at him. His sandy hair is cut short, and his blue eyes are the exact same shade as mine. They crinkle as he grins down at me. "You look beautiful as always," he says, taking in my paisley shirt dress and crisp ponytail. "How are you doing?"

My instinct is to lie. To tell him I'm fine, so he doesn't worry. He has enough stress, and I don't want to add to it any more than I already have. But Dad knows me too well. No doubt, he'd call my bluff. "I'm...hanging in there."

Understanding fills his eyes, and he runs a hand over my hair. "You've been dealing with a lot lately." He lets go of me and glances to where Carrie's watching us from the other side of the car. I was so excited to see my dad I didn't even notice her standing there. Dad waves her over.

"Hi, Quinn." Carrie smoothes her floral maxi dress as she walks over. Her shoulder-length brown hair is shiny in the street lights, and her smile is wide. I don't think I ever noticed how white her teeth are before. Something like nervousness lines her eyes, like she's worried I'm still mad at her.

I glance from Carrie to Dad. He's gazing at her with an expression of complete adoration. There's no way I could hold a grudge against a woman he looks at like that. I want my dad to be happy more than anything, so the smile on my face is real as I say, "Good to see you, Carrie. Welcome to Rosedale."

"It's good to see you. This town is just so charming." She motions around the street, filling with people on their way to the park.

"I love it here," I agree.

"So, hun." Dad swallows, looking suddenly nervous. "We have some news. And we think it will make your life a whole lot easier."

My forehead crinkles. "What kind of news?"

Dad puts an arm around Carrie's waist, pulling her to him. "Carrie and I are engaged."

My eyes fly open, and I press a hand to my mouth as a gasp of surprise escapes. "Engaged? Wow." I'm stunned. I knew things were getting serious between them, but I certainly didn't realize they'd gotten that serious. A shockwave of emotion hits me: astonishment, fear that I won't ever have a good relationship with Carrie, sadness that Dad's will be married to someone other than my mom. It's going to take time to sort through it all. But what I feel above anything else is genuine joy for my dad. He deserves to be happy.

I want them to know how much I mean it, so I force enthusiasm into my voice as I say, "That's amazing! Congratulations."

"Really?" Carrie bites her lip like she can't believe I could put the past behind us so easily.

"Really."

"Oh, thank goodness." She crushes me in a hug. It catches me off-guard, but I recover quickly, hugging her back. "I feel just awful about what happened, and I'd love it if we could start over."

"I'd like that too," I say as she releases me.

Dad rests a hand on my shoulder and clears his throat. "So, one of the many wonderful things about Carrie agreeing to marry me is that she's going to put us on her insurance. Her coverage is a lot better than what my company offers. It's going to pay for the costs of all your medications."

I blink at him. I'm so far past the point of being shocked I can't even form a sentence. I've been living in a constant state of panic over my healthcare expenses for such a long time. The idea that it could all be over is too good to be true.

Dad leans down to my eye level like he wants to make sure I understand what he's saying. "According to the law, you can stay on our insurance until you turn twenty-six. All your medical costs are going to be covered until then. Hopefully, that will give you enough time to get that nutrition business of yours up and running."

I take a shuddering breath. I'm shook by all their life-altering surprises. All I can think to say is, "That sounds like a pretty great law."

Dad and Carrie both laugh. An ember of hope ignites inside me, but worry snuffs it out before it can catch.

"Wait. You aren't getting married because of me, are you?"

"Oh, sweetheart, no." Dad shakes his head. "I proposed last weekend. Carrie knew about your situation, so she talked to her benefits department first thing Monday morning. We just wanted to wait and tell you in person."

"It's true," Carrie insists, nodding.

I look back and forth between them as the weight of all my financial stress topples from my shoulders, shattering against the cobblestone street. "Well, that's just really good news," I say, voice flooding with tears. Having my medical expenses taken care of means I'll be able to launch my business. I won't need to skip doses of my medication because I can't afford it. My health isn't going to spiral out of control again. Relief washes through me, and I break down in sobs in the middle of the street. I bury my face in my hands, and Dad and Carrie wrap their arms around me, holding me as I cry.

"Everything's going to be alright," Dad whispers against my hair. I nod, and for the first time in years, I believe it will be.

"Um, I hate to interrupt, but is everything good over here?" I turn to see Betty and Liv hovering next to us, looking both concerned and surprised. I'm sure seeing me hugging Carrie is unexpected, especially since I'm bawling my eyes out.

I scrub the heel of my hand across my cheeks. "Y-yeah." I stammer, trying to reign in my emotions. "Dad and Carrie are getting married."

Betty glances from my tear-stained face to Dad and asks, "And we're happy about that?"

"Very happy." I bob my head.

Betty breaks into a smile. "Okay, then. Congratulations!" She gives Carrie and Dad each a hug, but Liv's still watching me uncertainly.

"I'll tell you everything later," I say to her. "But I promise it's all good. Great, actually."

She lifts an eyebrow like she isn't sure if she should believe me. "Alright, but I want every single detail."

"Deal." I run my fingers under my eyes and over my cheeks. "Jeez. I'm probably such a mess." My face is wet with tear tracks, and I'm sure my makeup's wrecked. Not exactly how I wanted to look when I'm about to declare myself in front of the entire town. But I don't have time to do anything about it now. The sun's setting, and we need to get this show on the road.

"Nah. You look perfect. Real. This is, like, Quinn unfiltered."

I snort. "Right."

"Did you see that Paula's here?" Liv asks, jerking a thumb back toward the park.

"What? No." I spin around. Paula's standing behind the refreshment table. She's got one arm around Giselle's waist as she chats with the Reddys. I had no idea she was going to be here. I wonder how her mother's doing and who's staying with her.

"I'll find you after the movie starts," I say, and Liv nods. I glance over at Betty, Carrie, and Dad, but they're deep in a conversation about wedding details. I turn on my heel and practically bounce as I cross the road. I feel lighter than I have in a long time. I can't keep the smile off my face as I try to edge my way through the people swarming the table to pick out popcorn balls.

Paula spots me and grins. "Quinn! Get over here." She motions for everybody to let me through and gives me a big hug. "Thank you so much for all your hard work. Giselle told me what a fantastic job you've done, and this looks incredible. I owe you."

"It wasn't a big deal," I say. The festival tore through my life like a tornado this week. But that had more to do with the fact that I was running it with Ty than the events themselves.

Paula tilts her head, giving me a look. She obviously doesn't believe a word I'm saying.

"Okay, it was a lot of work," I admit. "But I'm happy I could help. How's your mom doing?"

"She's...okay." Paula holds up a hand, twisting it side-to-side in a so-so gesture. "She's still in quite a bit of pain. She's got a long recovery ahead of her, but she'll get there. My brother flew in from San Francisco to stay with her for the weekend, so I could be here."

"I'm so glad you could make it. The festival hasn't been the same without you."

"You've done just fine." Paula gives a dismissive flick of her wrist, but then her expression sobers. "Giselle did mention something about a poll for the movie, though."

I cringe, certain she's about to tell me off for nearly talking every-one out of coming tonight.

"You knew the movies listed in the binder were just the ones the rental company had available, right? They weren't all appropriate options for a family event. I thought you'd pick The Secret Life of Pets or something."

"Um, no." My teeth tug at my lip as my face heats. "We did not realize that." In hindsight, we should have, but Ty and I were so determined to outdo each other we weren't paying close attention to the details.

Paula shakes her head, but she chuckles. "Well, it never hurts to liven things up once in a while. I'm still eternally grateful for your help. Make sure to pass my gratitude on to Ty for me." She glances pointedly behind me.

The air leaves my lungs, and I slowly turn. The hum of conversation around the park ceases to exist. The caramel scent of Giselle's popcorn balls evaporates. I'm entirely unaware of anyone or anything else as my eyes land on Ty.

He's leaning against the gazebo, scanning the crowd. He looks so good it makes everything inside me ache. His dark hair is rumpled like he's recently run his hand through it, and his tan skin is warm against his black t-shirt. He's as heart-wreckingly gorgeous as ever. Looking at him is like reliving all my favorite memories: first kisses and summer nights. If he doesn't want to give us another chance, it will destroy me. But I know how lucky I am to have gotten to know him in ways no one else has. Whatever happens now, I'll always have the history of us.

Ty must sense my eyes on him because his gaze barrels into mine like a car in a high-speed collision. The impact knocks me sideways. Before I can gather my wits enough to wave, he looks away, mouth flattening into a hard line.

The air goes out of me, and my shoulders drop. Clearly, he's still mad at me. I'm not surprised, but I'd be lying if I said it didn't have me second-guessing my plan. It's nerve-wracking enough to tell someone you love them and want to be with them. Having to do it when they won't even look at you is terrifying.

"I think just about everyone's here," Paula says, bringing me crash-landing back to the present. "We should probably get started."

I attempt to shake off the doubts trying to devour me from the inside out, but my voice trembles as I say, "R-right."

Paula scrutinizes me, brows lowered in confusion. "Did you want me to give the welcome speech?"

"No!" The word comes out so forcefully that it catches Paula by surprise. Her head jerks back, and I wince. I didn't mean to snap at her, but I have to be the one to announce the movie. I try to reel in my obvious distress before she decides I can't be trusted to speak in front of everyone. "I already planned what I was going to say."

"Alright, then." Paula shrugs, but uncertainty lines her features. "Knock 'em dead."

I nod and take a second to rally my courage before turning toward the gazebo, ignoring the feeling of imminent danger threatening my heart.

Chapter 30

Ty's eyes are fixed on the ground as I walk over to him. His throat bobs, and I can tell he's fighting to control some kind of emotion. I'd give anything to know what's going through his mind. Because it doesn't feel like I'm wearing my heart on my sleeve so much as dangling it over a cliff. All I can do is put it out there and brace for the impact.

"Hey." I aim for an easygoing tone and miss. My voice is practically a croak. It's impossible to tell whether or not Ty noticed. He gives me the most cursory of nods but doesn't say anything.

It's all I can do to keep my feet from doing a one-eighty and running to the safety of the pool house. But I know if I don't risk it all and tell him how I feel, I'll always regret it.

"Should we get this party started?" I ask, forcing myself to sound upbeat even though I can hardly breathe through the dread pooling in my stomach.

"Yep." Ty doesn't look at me, but I take any verbal communication as a good sign. It's a low bar, but I need to cling to any remaining shreds of positivity if I'm going to survive the next five minutes.

Ty turns on his heel and marches up the gazebo steps like he's going off to war. He might as well be stomping all over my heart. I can feel it crumbling inside me, but I do my best to pick up the pieces and hustle after him.

The crowd must be eager for us to start the movie because they burst into a round of applause, much more enthusiastic than the situation calls for. Liv whistles and Betty lets out a loud, "Ow, ow!" I spot the Rossi's sitting on a quilt toward the center of the park. Lucia catches my eye and shoots me a discreet wink and a thumbs-up.

A thrill of confidence spikes through me, but it's short-lived. I glance over at Ty, and my stomach sinks. His arms are crossed over his chest, and he stares blankly out at the audience. He shifts his weight from foot to foot like he's ready to bolt the second this thing is over.

I remind myself that the hard part's almost done. I just have to get through the next few minutes. Then I'll know if Ty and I have a future together or if we'll be left with nothing but memories.

My hands tremble as I step up to the microphone. My fear of public speaking is attempting to make a comeback, but I'm determined to see this through.

"Hello, Rosedale." My words are shaky and quiet, but you'd think I said them with all the bravado of a head cheerleader with the way everyone responds. They clap and holler, and their enthusiasm gives me courage. My voice is steadier as I say. "Thank you so much for being here tonight. It's a relief to see your faces. We were worried all our smack-talk about the movie options might have convinced you to skip the event this year."

There are some appreciative chuckles from the crowd. I peek over at Ty. A muscle in his jaw ticks, but he doesn't make a move toward the mic. Okay. Apparently, I'm doing this by myself.

I clear my throat. "We're so grateful to all of you for playing along and casting your votes—"

"Which movie won?" Gary shouts from his place in the front row, cutting me off.

"I'm getting there, Gary. I promise." I hold up a hand, and laughter trickles through the park. "But first, let's give a big thanks to Giselle for providing the amazing food for all the events." I take a step back from the mic and clap my hands together. Everyone follows suit, even Ty. He might be mad at me, but he's not a jerk. He cheers for Giselle along with everybody else as she takes a bow.

It doesn't look like Ty's about to take over this speech anytime soon, though. His feet remain firmly planted where they are. I'm sure forcing me to do this alone is his way of punishing me. I can't pretend that doesn't sting, but he's also unintentionally doing me a favor. Now, I can just say what I came here to say and see where we stand.

"We also wanted to thank you all for participating in the events. We hope you had a great time, but we'll very happily be handing the reigns back to Paula next year." I keep saying 'we' as though Ty and I have actually discussed any of this. We've barely said a word to one another, but almost no one else knows that. They clap, and Paula gives a little wave.

"And now, for the moment you've all been waiting for," I say, and a hush falls over the park. There's definitely a power in public speaking. Having everyone hanging on your every word is kind of neat. I could get used to it if it wasn't for the hurricane of butterflies in my stomach.

"I'm thrilled to announce that this year's film is one that's near and dear to me," I say. I can practically feel Ty rolling his eyes. I ignore him and push onward. "This movie's special to me because it's special to someone I love with my whole heart."

I look over at Ty. His expression is stone, and he's still gazing vacantly at the crowd. I'm sure he thinks I'm referring to Liv or Betty. I don't take my eyes off of him as I say. "In fact, I'm pretty sure I'm going to love this person for the rest of my life."

There are some 'awwwws' from the audience, even though I doubt they know what I'm talking about. Ty's eyebrows furrow in confusion, making it clear he doesn't either. But he also doesn't bother looking at me, which makes this simultaneously easier and a hundred times more impossible.

"Ladies and gentlemen," I say through the lump building in my throat, "we present to you...The Bourne Identity."

Ty's eyes finally snap to mine just as someone hits the lights, cloaking us in darkness.

The crowd erupts. I wonder if anyone else notices how much louder the boos are from everyone who voted for Ever After than the cheers from those who voted for The Bourne Identity. They're by far outnumbered. But it's hard to care when I just lobbed my heart at Ty and have no choice but to wait while he decides what to do with it.

I can't see Ty, but I can feel the weight of his gaze on me as I grab onto the railing and hurry down the steps. I walk around to the back of the movie screen, away from all the prying eyes. Very few people know what my little spiel was about, but I think I made it apparent that I was declaring my undying love for Ty. Whether he chases after me or disappears from my life again, I will probably want some privacy.

I lean against the screen, staring into the night. A few lighting bugs flitter between the trees. Seeing them here feels like a good omen. But the anticipation clamped around my chest is so intense, it's a wonder I haven't started hyperventilating.

Thankfully, Ty doesn't make me wait long. I hear the hush of shoes on the grass next to me, and I'm sure it's him even before he says, "I thought you said Ever After won."

I turn to face him as the movie starts, illuminating the edges of the screen and casting us in bright, flickering light. Shadows dance across Ty's face. His jaw's still set in a hard line. But there's an unmistakable glimmer of hope in his eyes that sends my heart soaring like a balloon in a wind storm.

"It did." I swallow down the deluge of tears threatening to escape. "But that was before I voted. I don't know if anyone told you, but if you help plan the festival, you get a thousand extra votes."

"Is that so?" Ty takes a step into me, so we're only a heartbeat apart.

"It is." I nod. "But I didn't vote for The Bourne Identity. I voted for you, Ty. If I had a million votes, I'd vote for you every single time."

Ty reaches out, and his fingers find mine. He laces our hands together, and his lips curve into a smile made of shooting stars and happy-ever-afters. "Did you mean what you said back there?"

"I meant every word." A tear streaks down my face as I set my palm against his cheek. He leans his forehead against mine, and we stand like that for a beat, breathing each other in. The familiar smell of his cologne floods me with so many memories it makes my head spin.

"I'm so sorry for not being patient. I should have waited for you to tell me about your mom when you were ready." I say. "Letting go of control and trusting in anyone is hard for me, but I should've believed in you. You deserve that much."

Ty rubs a hand over his neck, nodding. "I should've believed in you too, Quinn, and I should've told you what was happening. My mom said you stopped by yesterday." He laughs, but his voice is thick. "She also yelled at me for not telling you what was happening from the beginning." His hands drift to my waist, and he pulls me against him. "I just didn't know how to talk to you after everything that happened between us. And you didn't exactly seem happy to see me again."

I wince because he's right. I felt a lot of things when I saw Ty standing next to Betty's swimming pool last week, but happiness definitely wasn't one of them.

I twine my fingers behind Ty's neck. My thumbs graze the fine hairs there, and he shivers. Being open and making myself vulnerable is like stepping off a ledge without a safety net. But having Ty's arms around me after all that we've been through makes me want to believe he'll always be there to catch me. "It hurt too much seeing you and not being with you," I admit. "I'm still so in love with you."

I feel his breath hitch in his chest, and his eyes gleam with emotion. "I love you too. So, so much." His fingers trail up and down my spine, and he swallows. "But if I'm going to be in this, Quinn, then I'm all in. I need you to be sure this is what you want. I can't have you questioning everything and breaking up with me when I go back to California to finish school in the spring. I can't go through that again."

"I know. I can't either." I shake my head, and a few tears trickle down my face. I brush them away with my shoulder because I hate the idea of letting go of Ty for a second. "I'm all in too. I want to be with you always."

"Yeah?" Ty's voice is hopeful, and his eyes dance with so much joy and love. I can see my entire future in those eyes.

In answer, I stand on my tiptoes and press my lips to his. He runs his hand over my hair, and I pull him closer until there's not a gap of space anywhere between us. I never want to be apart again. Our lips move together, slow and sweet, like we have all the time in the world. And for the first time, I truly believe that we do.

Ty wraps his arms tightly around me and lifts me off the ground. I let out a whoop of surprise as he spins me around in a circle, kissing me until we're both laughing. I'm dizzy with happiness. I could live in this moment for all my life.

Ty gently sets me back down, pressing kisses to my cheeks and forehead. "We probably need to go back out there at some point." He sighs and jerks his head toward the movie screen. I'd gotten so caught up in him I forgot that all our friends and family members were sitting just on the other side.

"Right." I reach up and trace his lips with my fingertips. "We'll pick this up later?"

"You better believe it." Ty brushes the gentlest of kisses against my mouth and takes my hand. "You ready?"

"As long as you're holding my hand, I'm ready for anything."

Ty winks at me, pulling me after him and making everything inside me turn to mush. But before I can all-out swoon, the squealing of car tires echoes through the speakers, and Gary yells, "Go! Go! Go! They're right behind you!"

Apparently, he was the only person paying attention to the movie, though. The second Ty and I walk out from behind the screen holding hands, the park explodes with applause. Liv and Betty are actually jumping up and down. Paula wolf whistles. Jenny is all-out bawling, arms wrapped around Old Man Jenkins's neck, who just looks confused. Marco and Ty's sisters are clapping wildly, and Lucia blows the two of us a kiss.

"About freaking time," Francie hollers.

My face is so hot, I'm sure it's on the verge of bursting into actual flames. I'm ready to go hide behind the screen again, but when I look up at Ty, he's beaming at me.

"The people came for a show." He shrugs and raises an eyebrow in a question.

I narrow my eyes at him. "You're going to be the death of me, Ty Rossi." Embarrassment beats through me like a pulse, but I can't fight the smile creeping across my face. I give a tiny nod, and Ty crushes his mouth to mine, kissing me until I'm breathless and everyone's cheering.

"Have I mentioned that my dad's here?" I ask, gasping for air as we break apart.

"Are you serious?" The mischievous grin falls from Ty's face, replaced by a look of utter terror.

"You'll be fine." I give him a pat on the shoulder. "It's been years since the last time you got me arrested. He's most likely over it by now."

Ty groans, but he puts an arm around my waist and presses a kiss to my hair.

My watch buzzes against my wrist. I glance down and see a text from Janet.

Janet: At the end of the day, all we have is who we are and the people we love.

I couldn't agree more, Janet, I think as I take Ty's hand and lead him through the park toward my family. I know I'll love Ty forever. Something tells me that no matter what obstacles we face in the future, we are always going to get back together.

Epilogue

I slide the binder across the table toward Paula, so she can see the meal plan I created for her. Thankfully, my nutrition binder is much smaller than her festival binder was. That thing would've put a hole right through Rossi's red-and-white-checked tablecloth.

Paula flicks through the pages, brows drawing together. My stomach is a jumble of anxiety as I watch. Paula's one of the first clients I've met with in person. I became a certified nutrition counselor a couple of months ago. Several people have signed up with me online already, but I still get nervous waiting to see people's reactions to the diets I recommend. Especially when they're sitting right in front of me.

I know what it's like to face the prospect of giving up your favorite foods. I hope to always add as many foods back into my clients' diets as possible once they're feeling well. But I remember how overwhelming it was to make those eliminations in the beginning. When Paula called me earlier this week and told me her doctor recommended she eliminate gluten and dairy, I could hear the uncertainty in her voice.

My toes tap inside my boots. I pick up my glass of ice water, take a gulp, and try to drown my nerves. Paula's still reading, so I force myself to look out the restaurant window just so I have something else to focus on. The leaves in the park have turned a fiery orange, and the street corners are decorated with towering corn husks, hay bales, and stacks of pumpkins. Summer may be my favorite season, but Rosedale is definitely at its most charming in the fall.

"It's hard wrapping my mind around the idea of not eating any gluten or dairy at all," Paula finally says, flipping the binder shut.

I nod in understanding. "Unfortunately, those are the two things that most commonly cause flare-ups in people with chronic conditions. If you're still struggling with your fibromyalgia in a few weeks, we can think about switching to the full AIP diet." Paula frowns uncertainly, and I hold up a hand. "But if you're feeling better, we can talk to your doctor and try adding something back in. Hang in there, and I promise we will get your diet optimized."

Paula's shoulders droop, but she slowly nods her head. "I like the sound of adding things back in, and I'll do just about anything to get rid of the pain at this point."

"I know the feeling." I smile sympathetically, hopeful that I'll be able to help Paula. I have the opportunity to make a positive difference in her health and overall happiness. I can't imagine doing anything more fulfilling.

"I'm assuming Nelson's triple-chocolate-chunk cookies are out of the question?" Paula slumps against the booth.

"Afraid so. At least for the time being. But," I lower my voice, leaning across the table toward Paula, "I've been working on a super-secret modified recipe. There's no gluten or dairy, and it's exclusively for my clients. You can't tell anyone, though. Shirley

Nelson would come for me if she knew I was messing with her cookie recipe."

"You're right about that." Paula laughs. "Alright, Quinn Kelley. You have yourself a client. These recipes look incredible, by the way." She pats the binder. "Are you teaching any classes on them?"

A smile streaks across my face. "I sure am. Swing by the school. I'm happy to give you some pointers if you'd like."

My classes at Giselle's have grown in popularity since I started my modifications course. I made enough money teaching over the summer to pay for my business insurance and licenses. I've also kept up with the Instagram live streams, which have helped me grow my platform to the point where sponsors actually pay me to use their products. When I think about where I was a few months ago, I can hardly believe how far I've come. I'm helping people change their lives for the better, and I'm making a living doing it. It's everything I ever wanted.

"I'll do that." Paula stands and offers me her hand. "Thank you for all your help. I feel like we're going in the right direction with this."

"My pleasure." I stand and shake her hand. "Feel free to call or text anytime if you have questions."

"Absolutely." Paula grins at me before turning and walking out the front door of Rossi's.

I collapse into the booth, sighing in relief and elation. That went better than I dared to hope. I spent the past week prepping for my session with Paula researching fibromyalgia. I'm optimistic about my plan for her, but I was still a nervous wreck over pitching it. Liv had to give me an hour-long pep talk over FaceTime last night, even though she was supposed to be studying for her midterms.

Speaking of which, I promised Liv I'd give her an update the second Paula and I finished. I pull my phone out of my tote bag and text her.

Me: I officially have a new client!!!!

Liv must've been waiting for my message because she responds instantly.

Liv: Duh. Of course, you do. So excited for you!

Liv: Now, please stop trying to save the world and do something useful...like planning what we're doing for fall break.

Liv's coming home next week, and I can't wait. Betty even made an advent calendar, counting down the days until she gets back.

Me: All over it.

Liv: You better tell Rossi I demand your undivided attention for the ENTIRE week.

I scoff. There's no way I'm going a whole week without seeing Ty. We spent too much time apart already, but I'm sure he'll happily participate in the activities Betty and I have planned.

Me: I have two words for you. Cannoli Saturday.

Betty decided Lucia and Ty's cannolis were worth breaking the alliterative activity theme for. Liv seems to agree. She replies with three running girl emojis.

"Refill?" Francie walks over, holding a pitcher of water.

"Please." I push my cup toward her.

"So, how'd it go?"

"Really well." I can't stop smiling as Francie fills my glass.

"I'm not surprised. You helped Mama so much. She's doing great." Francie sets the pitcher down on the table and leans against the booth. She's been working all day. Her feet are probably exhausted. Francie only wears shoes that have at least a three-inch-high heel.

"I can't take credit for that, but I'm so glad she's doing better." While I hope the dietary changes have helped Lucia feel her absolute best, the combination of surgery, radiation treatments, and hormone replacement therapy saved her. She's officially cancer-free.

"Uh-oh. That doesn't look like it's going at all well." Francie is zeroed in on a spot over my shoulder. I turn, following her gaze to a table on the opposite side of the restaurant.

Kallie Peters has her back pressed against her chair. Her arms are crossed tightly over her chest. It looks like she's trying to get as far away from the guy she's sitting with as possible. I can't blame her. Someone could have ordered him straight out of a bro catalog. He's got bleached blond hair, overly-tanned skin, and he's wearing a pastel pink polo shirt with the collar popped. Ew.

"So then I'm like, 'Dude, you can't tap a keg with an air compressor.'" Frat boy laughs loudly, smacking the table and making the glasses rattle.

Kallie raises an eyebrow and takes a long drink of her water.

"Yikes," I say to Francie. "Bad date?"

"Yup. Her third this week, too, which is all my sister's fault."

"Which sister?" I wrinkle my forehead. I have no idea how Lisa or Gianna could possibly be responsible for the train wreck happening in this dining room.

"Gianna, of course." Francie rolls her eyes. "She was at the salon getting her hair done and talked Kallie into letting her set her up. Gianna lined up ten different blind dates for her."

"Oof." I wince. "That sounds painful."

"That's what I said, but Gianna's, like, physically incapable of not meddling in other people's love lives."

I watch Kallie glare at her date and fondly shake my head. "Gianna's just a hopeless romantic."

"She's hopeless, alright."

The bell above the front door jangles, and Al walks in, holding hands with a middle-aged woman with red hair. He spots me and lifts his hand in a wave.

I grin and wave back. His whirlwind romance with Aunt Betty fizzled out after a couple of weeks, just as Liv predicted. I'm glad he found someone new. Al's a good guy.

"I should go. Duty calls." Francie nods to the hostess stand where Al and his lady friend are waiting. "But please, go pull my brother away from the computer before that big head of his implodes."

"Gladly." I smile and scoot out of the booth. It's been months since Ty and I got back together, but my heart still flutters every time I think about him. I'll never get enough of that boy. He's been buried in midterms this week, which he's doing online from home. I'm always more than happy to provide him with ample opportunities for distraction.

But before I can give Ty a good reason to take a study break, there's something I need to do first. I wind my way through the tables to Kallie. The rich, cheesy aroma of her manicotti has me practically drooling, but she hasn't taken a single bite.

Kallie wrinkles her nose as her date slurps up a plate of spaghetti while watching a video on his phone.

"Um, Kallie?" I ask.

"Dude! You've got to see this," her date says through a mouthful of un-chewed pasta.

Kallie slowly shakes her head and looks up at me. "Hey, Quinn."

The guy she's with smacks the table again, barking out a loud laugh and making Kallie and me jump.

Kallie presses her fingertips to her temples like his obnoxiousness is giving her a headache. She's in desperate need of saving. Luckily for her, I happened to pack my superhero cape today.

"So, Francie just told me your mom called the restaurant looking for you," I say.

"What?" Kallie squints her eyes in confusion. "Why would she call here? She knows I have my phone."

I turn my back to her date and shoot her a wink. I didn't need to have bothered, though. He's so engrossed in his video that he doesn't notice.

Understanding dawns over Kallie's face, and her eyes widen in relief.

"Yeah," I continue. "I guess someone accidentally dyed Jenny's hair blue."

"Oh, no." Kallie darts a glance across the table. "I should probably go help."

I nod. "I think they need you."

Kallie grabs her bag off the seat next to her and stands.

Her date finally glances up from his phone. "Are you leaving?"

"Yep." Kallie shoves her arms into her jacket and flips her long, caramel-colored hair over her shoulder.

"So what? You're just going to ditch and leave me to pay for your food?"

"Sure am." Kallie doesn't even look back at him as she hurries past me, squeezing my arm and muttering, "Thank you," under her breath.

"Anytime," I say to her retreating back.

"So, how about you then?" The guy looks me up and down like I'm a dish on an all-you-can-eat buffet. Ummm, gross much?

"Excuse me?"

"Wanna have lunch with me?"

I blink at him, dumbfounded that anyone could truly be that oblivious. "No."

"Your loss." He shrugs and turns his attention back to his phone.

I spin on my heel and shimmy my shoulders, trying to shake off the icky after-taste of my interaction with Kallie's date. I need to have a serious chat with Gianna about these guys she's setting Kallie up with. No girl should ever be subjected to that.

Francie shoots me a thumbs up, which I return as I make my way through the restaurant. It's nearly empty at this time of the afternoon. I push open the swinging doors that lead to the kitchen and wave to Marco. He's in the middle of explaining how to roll pasta dough to his new line cook. He calls hello, and I walk through the office door next to the big commercial refrigerators.

I pause, lean my head against the doorframe, and watch as Ty rakes a hand through his hair. He leaves it all tousled. His cheeks are flushed, and his eyes are glassy with fatigue. He's so focused on the computer screen he doesn't see me standing here.

"Hey there, handsome. You look like you could use a break."

Ty finally glances over at me, and his face lights up in a smile that makes me melt. "Wow, are you ever a sight for sore eyes." He holds his hands out to me, and I edge my way around the desk to sit on his lap.

I wrap my arms around his neck, tucking myself against him. "That seems like a very popular opinion this afternoon."

Ty's eyes narrow. "What do you mean?"

"Gianna set Kallie up on a date with a real winner out there." I jerk my thumb toward the dining room. "He was even sweet enough to ask me to take Kallie's place after she ditched him."

Ty pinches the bridge of his nose. "That sister of mine causes more devastation with her matchmaking than an iceberg in the path of the Titanic."

"Her heart's in the right place." I press my lips against Ty's warm cheek, and he hums happily.

"I wonder if Kallie agrees with that."

"Probably not. But if I remember correctly, Gianna was the one who set us up back in high school."

Ty's hands trail across my sides and over my hips, making me tingle all the way down to my toes. "True. But given the number of couples she's attempted to hook up, one was bound to stick eventually."

"Well, I'm grateful we were the lucky ones." I lean in and kiss him. The stubble on his chin is rough against my skin, but it doesn't bother me in the least.

"I couldn't agree more." Ty pulls me closer, kissing me until my mind goes deliciously fuzzy. I almost forget that his dad's standing right outside the open door. Almost.

I pull back, pushing myself off Ty's lap. My legs wobble, and Ty reaches out to steady me. He smirks, knowing full well that he's the cause of my weak knees.

I reach for his hands. "Come on, mister. Let's get you away from the computer."

A mischievous glint sparks in Ty's eyes. "Are you sure? Because we could close that door, and..." He waggles his eyebrows.

I laugh. "You really must've overworked your brain if you think any," I waggle my own eyebrows, "is happening with your dad out there." I tilt my head toward the kitchen, which is bustling with the sound of clanging pots and simmering sauces.

"Fine." Ty heaves a sigh and lets me pull him to his feet. He bends down and presses one last thorough kiss to my lips. "To be continued later?" he asks.

I grin up at him and take his hand. "To be continued always."